VALLEY OF DEATH

When Chad Chandler was close enough to hear the NVA making careless, metallic scraping noises—they were apparently preparing a nighttime snack—he leaped to his feet and charged down the hillside, screaming war cries and firing a carbine in each hand on full automatic.

Bright white tracers exploded with showers of sparks, startling the Asians and adding to the terror and confusion.

When he ran out of ammo, Chandler swung his rifles back and forth as he raced down the valley trail. Jaws and arm bones cracked in the pitch-black darkness.

And then a strand of barbed wire caught his lower leg, gouging into the flesh, and he tumbled over a mound of sandbags as a flare shot skyward, illuminating the killing zone. . . .

THE SAIGON COMMANDOS SERIES
by Jonathan Cain

NIK-UHERNIK

WAR
DOGS
#4
BODY COUNT

ZEBRA BOOKS
KENSINGTON PUBLISHING CORP.

ZEBRA BOOKS

are published by

Kensington Publishing Corp.
475 Park Avenue South
New York, NY 10016

First printing: May 1986

Printed in the United States of America

Dedicated to Tennessee Sheriff Buford Pusser.
He relentlessly pursued the mobsters of McNairy County,
unselfishly sacrificing his life in the endless war against the
evil that men do. He was one of the last true heroes. . . .

Show me a hero
and I will write you a tragedy.
                    — F. Scott Fitzgerald

"You can not hold onto a free press if it behaves irresponsibly. The idea that our mission is so high that no one should question our performance is illogical. The higher the mission, the more responsibly we should carry it out."

— Barry Bingham Sr.
Former chairman
of the International
Press Institute

1

Portland, Oregon

Fog choked the neighborhood for miles. Street lights were but a dim glow in the sky, their exact height above the street impossible to tell. A police car cruised by slowly. The emergency light on its roof sent lazy, crimson beams slicing through the silver gauze.

The squad car was on an emergency run, but the weather conditions made speed impossible. It soon vanished in the slowly moving wall of haze. There was no other traffic on the street at such a late hour.

The man sitting in the white 1964 Plymouth Fury sipped on a steaming cup of coffee, and slid his elbow along the inside of the door, checking the lock— making sure it was secure. He glanced over his right shoulder, but the street was still deserted. The officer in the police car had not even noticed him probably.

He set the styrofoam cup on the dashboard, started

the engine and lit a cigarette. The man revved the motor lightly a couple times, turned the heater fan up full blast until the car filled with warmth again, then shut everything back off and continued watching the third-floor window across the street.

Two men in their early twenties, white, and wearing jeans and black leather jackets, appeared down at the end of the block. Their hair was short, the man in the Plymouth observed, but they were both obvious street toughs who hadn't bathed or changed clothes for days.

He watched them glance nervously up and down the block, then walk up to the apartment house and test the seal of several ground-floor windows before finding one that was unlocked.

Prying with grease-caked fingers, the two quickly had the window open. There was no screen at all. *Low rent district,* the man in the Plymouth thought to himself as he settled back to watch the burglars climb into the apartment. He quickly put out his cigarette and slid down in his seat, curious why they had not "made" him long ago. *Probably doped up,* he decided, grinning.

There was a dim light burning inside the room, and even at this distance he could make out the bed against the far wall. Before the drapes fell back in place, he watched them rush toward the sleeping woman lying on her stomach atop some blankets. The woman was wearing only bikini bottoms—*a dull pink,* he guessed, at this distance. Her hair was long and blond and fanned across her back. But then there was a sudden movement on her part. *She must have sensed their presence in the room.* And as she sat up in the bed, whirling around, her breasts swung to the side heavily, then back. He watched them jiggle about slightly as her eyes went wide, and he rolled the window down a crack in time to hear her muffled scream before they were upon her and the drapes fell back into place. Down the street, something metallic roared, straining.

A movement along the right edge of his peripheral vision caught his attention, and he turned to see a huge fire truck turning onto the block. Like the police car, its roof light twirled about slowly, shooting red beams of light through the blanket of fog like a hot knife through butter. And like the officer in the cruiser, the firemen had elected not to use their siren — the roar of the engine was enough to wake the dead of night.

The truck, a long hook-and-ladder affair, rushed past, and as the drapes of the apartment were thrown back again he saw one of the men holding the woman down while the other ripped the bikini bottom down across her hips, along her thighs and toward her ankles as she kicked her legs wildly, resisting.

As the blast of wind died away and the drapes fell back in place he rolled the window back up and pulled his jacket collar tight around his throat. Two more fire trucks rolled by, and when the drapes were blown aside he saw that one man still held the woman down by the wrists. His partner was on top of her now, though, pants down around his ankles, hips plunging back and forth madly, bending her neck against the headboard of the bed.

The man in the Plymouth felt no guilt as he shifted about in his seat and searched for another cigarette, ignoring the woman's plight totally — the scene had merely served as a temporary distraction. It was none of his business. Another muffled cry reached his ears, and he started the engine again and turned up the heater fan like before.

Then he resumed watching the window of the dark apartment on the third floor.

The soldier ran toward her, rifle raised high in one hand, as if in slow motion. His eyes were filled with terror, and his mouth was open, but no sound came from it. A stubborn, bluish mist grabbed at his ankles — many men in parkas with red stars on their helmets were chasing him through the snow.

Somehow she knew his rifle was empty, useless. She got the feeling she knew him from somewhere, but the name would not come to her — she could not focus on the face as a whole, only the eyes and mouth.

He was calling her name suddenly, over and over — the words reaching her as if from the bottom of a well, echoing. She reached out to him, but he seemed to be falling back, farther away, and she could not see her own hands in front of her.

And then one of the men in thick parkas was raising a tube to his shoulder and a brilliant flame flashed in front of his face. She watched the projectile chase after the man and explode against his back.

"Father!"

But the man had vanished in a surrealistic puff of smoke, and the soldiers standing in the distance were laughing without making any noise. And pointing at her. Pointing. Laughing and pointing. . . .

April Adams sat up in her bed, eyes wide with horror. Her chest was heaving and beads of perspiration covered her face.

For a moment she just sat there, trying to get her bearings. Her eyes darted about the room, but her limbs did not move. The only sounds were her labored breathing and a siren fading in the distance.

She rolled over to the edge of the bed suddenly, reached into the nightstand drawer and pulled out the small revolver. Then she slid across the blankets onto the floor, shaking — their "presence" was almost over-powering this time. And she began searching the apartment for the communist Chinese soldiers.

A couple minutes later, after checking the closets and under the bed and in the bathroom, she came to the door and saw that the lock had not been disturbed. There were no intruders in the room — no Red Chinese with bayonets on their rifles, coming to get her.

Just as she had almost calmed down she was "con-fronted" by the person in the hallway and she screamed, dropping the revolver on the carpet. But then she laughed, almost hysterically: it was only her reflection in the huge mirror.

"I . . . am . . . alone," she told herself quietly, as if

11

exorcising her private little ghosts. "There is nobody in this apartment but me. Me!"

She slowly dropped to one knee and picked up the gun, locking eyes with the woman in the mirror as she did. She was shocked by what she saw. The circles under the eyes, the hollowed cheeks, the disheveled hair—she reminded herself of what walking death must look like. And April Adams promised to start taking better care of the woman in the mirror.

She took the revolver back to the bedroom and slid open the nightstand drawer. Inside, the shiny .38 cartridges sparkled back at her. She laughed aloud again, tossing the weapon in beside the bullets and slamming the drawer shut—the damn gun hadn't even been loaded. She sat down on the edge of the bed and dropped her face in her hands. *And what good would it have done against my midnight ghosts anyway?* she sobbed silently.

The slim, seventeen-year-old girl sat there for several minutes, then finally summoned the strength to look up at the wall clock: four a.m., the luminous arms glowed back at her in bright green. Puffs of fog pressed against the third-floor windows, peeking in at her. They made her shiver, and she pulled the nightgown collar closer . . . tighter.

April whisked her long, reddish-brown hair over one shoulder and commanded her legs to take her off the bed. Taking in a deep breath of air, she glided over to the record player and turned it on, careful to keep the volume dial low before the set warmed up. Its arm

12

automatically tracked across with a light clicking noise, and the needle set down on a Buffy Sainte-Marie album.

As the Cherokee Indian singer's haunting tune, "Sweet September Morning," filled the dark room, April moved to the kitchen and put a small tea kettle on the gas stove. As it warmed, she took a small red box of Chinese Restaurant tea from the cabinet and set it on the counter, then returned to the small living room.

She removed her nightgown, draped it over a strawlike Oriental rattan chair and sat on the wood floor. She was naked from the waist up now—baggy GI shorts bought during a sale at the Army surplus store across the street hugged her hips—and she shivered as the coolness in the apartment rubbed in on her from all sides.

She quickly began the stretching exercises, humming to the song in the background, and as she bent forward and back, forward and back, the tips of her nipples brushed against her thighs, warming her, chasing the cold back into the corners.

Her breasts, full and firm, refused to flatten out entirely as she shifted her legs out wider and commenced falling forward until her chest rubbed against the hard floor. April Adams was not concentrating on her figure, however. She did not even realize how beautiful and attractive she really was, how many of her male "friends" lusted for her silently, fantasized about her privately.

13

Her thoughts were entirely on the man in her dream — her nightmare — and how she had never been able to clearly see his face. As her favorite song on the album, "The Surfer," came on, she shifted into more rigorous exercises, and her momentum seemed to switch to future goals: a successful singing and dancing career, fame . . . fortune.

But her eyes remained moist and sad as she stared up at the faded photograph on the mantle above the phony fireplace. The picture, showing her mother and father standing in front of a waterfall somewhere in Colorado, was out of focus and cracking, but it was the only one she had. The man's face was a blur, a lost memory.

April Adams continued to sing along softly with the words coming from the record player, and as the song became "Los Pescadores," she continued humming in a frightening, singsong tone that did not seem her own. She did not know what the words filling her private little torture chamber of memories were saying, but neither did she understand anything that had happened in her life since they had taken her mother to the "hospital" after her father had disappeared.

For years they had told her he was dead, but now she was almost grown, almost an adult, ready to really strike out on her own, and the dreams that came to her on gloomy nights like this told her they were all wrong.

Somewhere, her father was alive. Living another life perhaps, but alive.

She prayed he was waiting for her.

14

* * *

The man in the white Plymouth poured another cup of coffee from the thermos and sat back to watch the ground-floor window across the street.

The eastern horizon was as dark as ever, hidden by the fog bank, but a feeling in the air told him a pre-dawn light lingered beyond the thinning haze.

An overnight express bus rushed past, and the tailwind chasing it blew the drapes of the apartment aside. The two men were off the woman now, and the arm of one was winding back and forth, back and forth, plunging a blade down into her chest as her legs, spread apart and sprinkled with blood, kicked out wildly.

The man in the Plymouth rolled the window back down a crack, but he heard no screams, and as the drapes fell back in place he knew the woman on the bed was no longer resisting.

Damned high-crime neighborhoods, he muttered to himself, glancing back up at the third-floor apartment window as he took another sip of coffee and the burglars crawled from the ground floor room. *Nobody even calls the cops anymore.* He took another sip of the steaming brew, keeping his eyes on the third-floor window. One dim light had come on. *They oughta activate the National Guard and wipe out the whole block, using an artillery battalion.*

The man frowned. He knew he would have to act fast if he was to contact the girl on the third floor before someone discovered the corpse and the joint was swarming with police. Then again, considering the neighborhood, a week could pass before the girl was missed, or the open window even noticed. Or the foul smell detected.

2

At a rain forest camp along the Vietnam-Cambodian border

The raging campfires were arranged in a semicircle before the stone palace that hung from the cliff wall and jutted up toward the tangled triple-canopy overhead. For hundreds of yards, trees had been toppled over the months, leaving a clearing that afforded the Khmer tribe ample space to live and work in harmony with the forces of the jungle. Somehow the snaking branches above remained intact, blocking out the stars, and though the fires lent a smoky haze to the grounds after dusk, they also kept back the wild animals and swarming bugs.

"January 1965!" young Cory MacArthur spoke with mock fury, and a tree monkey crashed through the branches overhead, fleeing in terror. "You couldn't bring back anything from Bangkok a little more current?"

Chad Chandler flexed his huge biceps and frowned down at the slender eighteen-year-old. "It's only a few months old." He sounded like he didn't care. "You're lucky I brought you back anything at all, shrimp!"

17

The words were spoken playfully, but the short American shot to his feet anyway, shaking himself free of the two golden Cambodian girls clamped to either arm. He pushed the muscular ex-mercenary backwards, off balance, then charged him — to the wide-eyed surprise of the teen-aged girls on the ground.

Chandler grunted — almost as if on cue — and the men tumbled through the elephant grass, wrestling.

It was a game they played — mostly for MacArthur's benefit. He had yet to latch onto a steady girlfriend at the camp, even though they had been living with Princess Raina's people for months now, nearly a year in fact. Cory would choose one (or sometimes two) young maidens from the hundreds available, romp around in the reeds with her (or them) for a few days (though he never seemed to spend the entire night with them — Matt Sewell maintained the kid was still a cherry boy, even after all these missions in the exotic Orient) then stumble into a fight in front of them, hoping to impress the girls with his courage and strength.

The Khmers were a people who respected cunning and bravery, even the young women. *Especially the young women,* Chandler had maintained over many a midnight campfire — and Cory often took to ruffling his tail feathers in front of them, anticipating the customary reward afterwards. But he had yet to brag to the others about any conquests, and the War Dogs all doubted there had ever been any.

A tall, agile, bronzed form flew from the treeline and appeared beside the two wrestlers, and the women in tight, one-piece sarongs knelt on bare feet behind the sharp reeds to watch.

18

"Awright, knock it off!" Justin Ross, clad only in khaki shorts and a gun belt, reached down and separated the men. "We got business to attend to!"

Still huffing and puffing for the benefit of the Khmer maidens, they directed their best heart-eating glares at the Army lieutenant and grudgingly rose to their feet. Smeared red across the chest from an accidental nosebleed, Cory dusted himself off as if he had enjoyed the match thoroughly, and cast the hiding eyes a confident wink. Then he gave Big Chad a friendly thumbs-up, and the two men followed Ross back to the longhouse-on-stilts at the edge of camp.

"We finally got a mission?" Chandler sounded anxious as he glanced at a hut several feet away, where a woman held a small, amber baby in her arms and his clothes hung from a drooping line outside a side window.

"Not quite," Ross muttered, handing the ex-merc a folded radio message that had been just recently decoded. "Old man Y back at the Big P says he's disturbed at the way we smoked that Congressman couple months ago at the old camp."

"Nobody's got a sense of humor anymore these days," MacArthur wiped the blood from his chest with his hands, then in turn wiped the fingers on his light brown pants. All three men were barefoot.

"He says we're to stand by for a second message sometime next week," Ross continued. "The shit has really hit the props with this Kennedy assassination commission pryin' open closets in search of skeletons, and he says we might be needed for some domestic jobs."

"Domestic?" Cory gave Ross a quizzical look.

19

"Stateside, stupid," Chandler answered for the lieutenant.

"I like it here, Justin," Cory stopped and opened his arms to the rain forest rising up all around them. "I don't wanna go back to The World," he said, despite the almost ominous, living-breathing power pressing in on the white men.

"Shit," muttered Chad Chandler, and the other two soldiers wondered if he was referring to Mr. Y or Cory's remark.

"I thought you maybe had some word from Amy." The kid did not think he was sounding weak now in mentioning the woman he had come to think of as his big sister.

"Amy?" Ross laughed aloud.

"What made you think that?" Chandler agreed the remark was a wasted wish.

"Well, all I've gotten from her in the last three weeks—"

"*You've* gotten something from her?" Ross sounded shocked.

"What did she send *you*?" Chandler grabbed Cory's arm, whirled him around and up against a tree, and began playfully frisking him. He came up with a colorful postcard stuffed down a back pocket.

"And I figured she'd at least keep *you* posted regarding where she was and what she was doing!" MacArthur raised his voice slightly.

"Not since I found that note in her hut the morning she left!" Ross grabbed the postcard from Chandler.

"And how the hell did you get a friggin' *postcard*?" Chandler folded his thick forearms across his chest as he leaned back over Cory in judgment. "All the way

20

out to this Christforsaken jungle outpost?"

"Some old papa-san on a rundown bicycle came pedaling along a few days ago, down that trail that runs along the river." Cory pointed, but Ross didn't seem to hear anything the youth said as he concentrated on the few words scribbled across the back of the card. "I guess he was the area mailman or something. He had a whole backpack filled with local parcels, and striped envelopes with airplanes and *Par Avion* stamped all over them were falling out from sacks tied to the handlebars."

The handwriting was hers. Ross frowned: not much more than a "doing just fine" and "wish you were here" to go on.

She had left three weeks ago.

The note said she was tired of watching Ross and his War Dogs eating Cambodian beaver day and night, and it was time for her to take a little R&R.

She had mentioned Manila. There are Latino-types that hang out there, the note had said. Maybe she could find a Filipino man to satisfy her, remind her she was still a woman, and not just a cold-hearted killer, assigned to a covert squad of mad-dog gunman.

Ross had gone after her of course.

Had intercepted her a few *klicks* on the other side of the Vietnamese border, on a bus headed for Tan Son Nhut airport. And they had talked it over until well past dusk.

Ross was nobody's fool. He knew Amy and Brent had been pumping each other since before the Diem hit. What puzzled him was their recent rift—he wondered what had come between them. The nagging suspicion was that it involved the chase and shoot-out

21

with the Wanda target, the terrible wounds she had sustained, the manner in which the war dogs had abandoned her to the dark, and the all-encompassing pain . . . the all-consuming hurt.

Collins had never confided in him, not the way men in the midst of a combat zone trust each other—he often went off on his own between missions. And Amy was worse. She never acknowledged the bond between them anymore, and her tone at briefings barely bordered on civil. She made her position clear to the others: she did not want to be here (did any of them?). Her tour of duty with the war dogs was involuntary—a death sentence, a life term from which there would be no pardon.

Hoping a few days away from the men would soften her up a bit, Ross had granted her the short R&R, even lending her some greenbacks. But he made it clear she was to be back in seven days—two weeks at the most—and that they'd come looking for her if she failed to return.

International travel was dangerous during these times of uncertainty, and when the deadline approached and passed, Ross made no immediate decisions. Mr. Y back at the Pentagon had yet to make contact about any new missions, so they were not hurting for time. That was one of the few good things about the team: that "lag time" between hits. It often lasted weeks. Sometimes months. And old man Y was not the type to harass them with busy work like raking dirt or painting stones. He was more than happy to let them lose themselves in the middle of a tropical rain forest, safely on the other side of the world, deep in darkest Asia. So Ross had sat back, watching the coconuts (and *his* nuts, the war dogs) grow, and done nothing.

Until now.

The message was in: another target was out there waiting for them to strike it down. As soon as they were given the green light.

He doubted they could make it to Manila and back in that amount of time—it would take twice as long just to track down his favorite little Guatemalan refugee. Ross examined the postmark, but it was nearly unreadable. He nodded his head from side to side. The Philippines had one of the worst postal systems in the world—he was surprised they had received the tiny card at all.

Parrots in the trees suddenly went silent, and both Chandler and Ross tensed from the experience, but no riflefire shattered the eerie calm—only rolling thunder that erupted in the north and seemed to rush across the highest layers of canopy, rattling the branches. Sheets of rain began falling, but the dense flora overhead prevented any water from reaching the people below, in the clearing.

"There she is again." Cory changed the subject as he motioned toward the treeline with a single finger without turning his head. The manner in which he pointed told Ross and Chandler they were not to be obvious when they sneaked a peek.

Tired of games, Ross turned his entire body in reply, but the spotted leopard standing between the two tamarind tree trunks did not flee back into the forest.

Man and beast locked eyes, and for a moment, nothing moved. Then the big cat roared against the

23

clamor of the approaching storm, arcing its head back and extending its jaws out as it did—but never taking its eyes off the Army lieutenant. Teeth bristling, the leopard screamed for several seconds without letting up, and Ross slowly drew the pistol from his holster.

"No," Cory whispered harshly.

But as thunder crackled directly overhead and a bolt of lightning struck down a tree a thousand yards distant, the leopard vanished in the split-second that ages-old fear distracted the men, drawing their eyes to the skies and the gods that hid and laughed beyond the triple canopy above.

"Whadda ya mean 'no'?" Ross slowly reholstered his .45 and took his eyes from the collage of browns and greens closing in on them from all sides. "What the hell is this goofy love affair you got with that overgrown pussycat, anyway?"

"*I* wanna catch her," MacArthur rubbed the medicine man's pouch around his neck. "*I* wanna kill her myself and—"

"He wants to add her claws to his lucky bag there," Chandler explained. "Sewell told him it would make for powerful medicine."

"He said I gotta kill her with my bare hands," the youth admitted. "African style—like the wildmen in Zululand do."

"That's all a crock o' shit." Big Chad put into words what Justin Ross was thinking.

"You just want to string up a tiger-claw necklace." The team leader grinned. "It's the rage among soldiers these days, you know." His accent took on a Beverly Hills twang.

"If he's not careful—" Chandler's eyes scanned the

24

rain forest for any sign the big cat was still lingering out there somewhere— "he's gonna end up mush in that animal's belly."

Ross shook his head in the negative as all three men started back toward the stone palace. "The poor tiger'd die of indigestion!"

"Well I'll be a son of a . . . " Cory's words trailed off as he spotted the old man coasting down the jungle trail on his rickety bicycle. "It's the mailman I was tellin' you about, Justin!"

Several of the tribe's children ran up to greet the papa san as he pulled up in front of the longhouse at the edge of the clearing. He handed the tallest girl three crumpled letters with the local postage on them, then glanced about the smoky clearing until he spotted the approaching Americans.

His mouth became a toothy smile, and he handed a small, folded envelope to the nearest child and pointed at the Westerners.

Displaying no fear but an affectionate twinkle in her eyes, the five-year-old girl ran up to Ross and hugged his legs, dropping and completely forgetting about the cable in the process.

Chandler, frowning at the public display of emotion, bent down and retrieved the telegram while Ross picked the girl up and twirled her about over his head.

Squealing with delight, her excited cries brought the other children up to the men. Several of the village women appeared in the doorways to their huts, all smiling: these foreigners had long ago earned their respect and a place of high standing in the community. But Chandler, after handing his lieutenant the envelope, backed away from the noisy assemblage. Visions of slaughtered children suddenly filled his head, and his mind's eye saw a treetop sniper firing down at the clustered, unprotected targets—it had not been that long ago these same people were killed by the scores at a similar clearing only one valley away.

Ross began walking toward the stone palace as a woman in the longhouse called the bothersome children away, and Chandler and his younger charge followed.

"It's from Amy," the lieutenant announced as they approached the towering temples at the foot of the palace wall and they passed into the shadows.

"So read it." Cory was not watching the older soldiers, but the stone archway passing above their heads. Even after all these weeks, the centuries-old structure awed him, capturing his imagination, every time he approached it.

Princess Raina had moved her clan here shortly after the last big battle with the opium-caravan leaders. Ross and his men had arranged a truce of sorts with the renegade Chinese bandits, but no one was sure how long it would last. The princess had left a small band of her most trusted warriors behind at the old camp, so it wouldn't appear deserted, then moved the remainder of her followers home to sacred ground. Ross and his team had been startled at first when a bend in the jungle trail revealed the huge palace rising up from the mists in the vast, smoky clearing. Built into a high cliff wall with shale stones the color of gold, the structure rose nearly ten stories, and housed dozens of families in cliff-dweller-like orderly fashion. Armed sentries patrolled the topmost rim. At night, ladders allowing access to the bottom-most level,

26

twenty feet off the ground, were raised, and snipers were posted at strategic points across the clearing. Roving guards walked the smoky reeds, keeping the campfires roaring during the hours of darkness. After daybreak, they were allotted "penthouse" cubicles on the top story of the palace—a floor set aside for the bravest warriors, the princess herself, and honored visitors, such as Ross's team, though the Americans and the princess always stayed in the longhouse on the other side of the clearing, with the numerous members of her family. Raina shunned the isolation, power and influence that came with the being born into royalty—she prohibited her people from treating her differently than anyone else. And Raina was in love with Justin Ross.

"So what the hell does it say?" Cory MacArthur tugged on Ross's elbow as the three soldiers passed into the high-walled courtyard that stretched out between the palace columns and the jutting worship temples on the other side of the archway.

Ross came to a sudden stop upon reading something, and Cory, who had been smiling up at a young woman sitting in a third-floor window petting a tame gibbon, bumped into him from behind. Chandler frowned. *And I often place my life in his hands*, he thought, disturbed the youth could so easily be distracted by a pretty face.

"She's still in Manila," Ross finally said.

"Still in the Philippines?" Big Chad's tone was laced with growing irritation, like his day had already started out bad, and this could only add to his misery.

"Yeah? So when does she plan on coming back?" Cory asked sarcastically, and then he answered himself before Ross could speak. "Never, if she's got as much smarts as she's got chest."

"Seriously, Justin." Chandler pushed young Cory off balance and out of the way. "Has Amy run into some kind of problem? I been gettin' bad vibes ever since I saw that old man rollin' up on his bicycle." He didn't realize it was because the sight reminded him of a night back in Saigon, months earlier, when they were all together, dining at an open-air cafe on Le Loi, and a plastic-explosives-packed bike had been detonated right across the street, killing many Vietnamese browsing at the market, and showering their table with blood.

"She says she's in trouble," the lieutenant revealed, handing the cable to Big Chad. "Amy wants us to start packing our duffel bags for Manila. She needs our help fast!"

Portland, Oregon

The man was nearly as wide as he was tall, and the pre-dawn shadows lent a sinister shade that made him look twice as menacing as he left the white Plymouth sedan and started up the steps to the rundown apartment house. He was wearing a knee-length trench coat, pulled tight around the collar, and a hat that prevented most of his face from being seen. Not that anyone was watching the street at that hour.

The man walked quickly past the open window on the ground floor, never pausing to look in as the wind blew back the drapes as he flew by.

Before a minute had elapsed, he had climbed the dim inner stairwell and was rushing down the corridor of the third floor. He cocked his boxer's face to one side as the faint singing reached his ears, but he did not slow down until he was standing in front of her door.

He paused silently for several minutes then, staring alternately at the peephole and up at the numbers above it: 313. And he listened intently.

To the soothing tones behind the door: the innocent

voice of a young woman too pure to be dealing with animals the likes of himself.

A thick layer of black hair bristled along his knuckles as he tested the doorknob, but it was locked. He leaned forward, peering into the peephole the wrong way, but he could see nothing except the reflection of his own eyeball.

The humming voice grew louder, and he could feel her pass by on the other side of the door, then the soothing sound became faint and he listened to her step into the shower and turn on the water.

Fritz Glover shook his massive head from side to side. The old man downtown was choosing them younger and younger these days, he decided. But what business was it of his, really? The Organization paid him little enough as it was for his talents, so why ponder the morality of it all?

The Glove, as his back-alley buddies called him, glanced up and down the hallway, then pulled the stiletto from his front pants pocket. It shot open with a flick of a wrist, the blade gleaming in the dull light from a ceiling lamp at the end of the narrow corridor.

Glover slipped the knife into the door frame below the knob and lifted up through the jamb, expertly slipping the lock back. The apartment was not equipped with a deadbolt. He started to pull on the doorknob when he heard light footsteps suddenly running up the stairwell down at the end of the hallway.

His hand holding the knife shot down into the pocket of his trench coat moments before the newspaper boy appeared at the top of the steps.

The youth, loaded down with thick Sunday papers, skidded to a halt upon seeing the huge man and abandoned his earlier exuberance. He swallowed hard, but kept his chin set firm and glared up at the stranger before resuming his duties.

Fritz Glover's downcast head turned slowly, following the boy's every move as he passed. When he reached the adjoining apartment, the youth dropped a heavy newspaper on the floor in front of the door and backed down the hallway, never taking his eyes off the giant in the trench coat.

He dropped another paper in front of a door at the end of the corridor, then ran down a second, rarely used set of stairs leading to the rear of the building.

"Fucking brat'll probably run this town in twenty years," he muttered under his breath as he again produced the stiletto. "And I'll still be hustlin' little cherry girls for the Organization — all thanks to the free enterprise system."

The door slid open noiselessly. Running water could still be heard coming from the back of the apartment. The Glove glanced up and down the hallway a second time, then tiptoed into the room and closed the door softly behind him.

With the seven-inch blade poised level with his beltline, Glover walked slowly toward the bathroom, cautiously glancing in the rooms he passed through to get there, but the girl was alone. Just as the boss had said she would be.

A fine mist hung in the air as he slowly opened the bathroom door. Glover smiled broadly: she had not

31

locked it.

No screams greeted his entrance, like he expected. The woman's eyes were closed as she lathered her hair with shampoo. Water from the hot shower ricocheted off her shoulders. The tiny room was quickly fogging up.

She hesitated for the slightest moment as he closed the bathroom door behind him — perhaps sensing a change in the room temperature — but then she went back to turning in the shower, soaping every inch of herself down. Her eyes remained tightly shut the entire time.

Glover moved closer and peered over the shower curtain. His smile returned and the blade in his hand slowly went up, but then he remembered where he was, and what he was doing — he bit his lip, regaining control, and folded up the stiletto.

The old thug felt suddenly blessed — privileged, in fact, that he should be able to view such a young, unblemished body. April Adams' skin was as smooth as satin. The soap suds refused to cling to any joints or hollows, and the water itself seemed to trickle away from the skin as if flowing down a flawless statue made of wax. He wondered if he was seeing things. Perhaps walking around in all the fog outside, then directly into a bathroom where the shower was in use altered one's senses.

He did not really care. He felt himself growing uncontrollably hard.

Her breasts were firm and youthful, jutting straight out against the flow of water. The nipples, taut and erect, seemed to stare back at him like earth-red whirls as she turned slightly.

The boss's no-nonsense scowl flashed in front of Fritz Glover's face just then, and his smile faded. He quietly backed out of the room and closed the door.

A second later, the shower was turned off. Water could be heard swirling down the drain. Plastic slid across metal as the curtain was pulled back.

"Is anybody there?"

Her voice was a pleasant surprise, and Glover smiled again as he returned to the living room—not because of her apparent naivete at the choice of words over *"Who's out there?"* but because her tone was so innocent, so childlike, so vulnerable.

The Glove sat down in a plush couch and glanced about the living room. It was furnished in ancient Oriental design. The Sainte-Marie album's final song filled the apartment, and after a tense silence, the girl in the shower began humming along with the soft, drawn-out chords.

Glover sighed as he took in the plastic surroundings. Not bad, for a dame who wasn't out of diapers yet. Asian tapestries the size of tablecloths hung from all four walls. They were large, but he recognized them as the cheap kind you could buy at the Indian bead shop downtown for four dollars a toss. Black stone Manchu statues rose from wooden pedestals in every corner, and dragons that looked like ivory but were really carved from water buffalo horns sat atop the small black-and-white TV and a narrow desk. "Jade" figurines on a shelf running along one wall were actually

33

fashioned from simple glass. But all of the items taken together, combined with the set of black bamboo drapes that separated the bedroom from a hallway, lent a definite Far Eastern flavor to the dwelling. *All she needs is a little joss smoke,* Glover decided, his nose wrinkling at the thought—floating incense irritated him.

He glanced about the room a second time, searching for telltale clues a man also lived here, but there were none, and he wondered why an American woman was so attracted to Oriental culture—or a cheap imitation of it. He had been to Hong Kong a couple times, and had always thought of Asia as a man's private playground.

He had actually started thinking back to the long-haired Wanchai woman with her legs spread, lying on her back in the bowels of the Chinese junk at Aberdeen harbor, when the girl entered the living room and shrieked.

"My God! *Who are you?*"

She had just wrapped a wine-red towel around her hips, and her breasts danced in front of his eyes again, jiggling about as her feet skidded to a halt.

Their eyes met, and she froze—totally at a loss as far as what her response should be.

Fritz Glover remained seated, but his eyes dropped to her moist, ample chest. "April Adams?" he asked without any emotion whatsoever.

Her hands rose to cover her breasts, and the towel fell loose, fluttering to the floor.

April sprang behind a chair, which did little to

conceal her sumptuous curves. "Who are you?" she demanded. "How did you get in here?" But her tone did not fool Glover. Tears were welling up in the girl's eyes. She was terrified.

"The door was unlocked," he lied coldly. "I knocked, but there was no answer. I could hear the shower. I didn't want to disturb you, so I just made myself at home. I hope you don't mind." His head dipped slightly and he made his eyes look like a sad, defenseless cow's as he glanced up at her.

April's legs bent at the knees as she reached out for the towel. Her breasts bounced about and swayed from side to side, and her crotch opened itself up to him for a moment, arousing the burnt-out hood in the trench coat again. Glover shifted his eyes to the tapestry of children walking on a water buffalo's back somewhere in the Gulf of Siam, but his mind was seeing young April Adams stretched out on the floor, her legs spread wide, straining to wrap themselves completely around him as he thrust into her, over and—

"I demand to know who you are!" She finally reached the towel and held it up to her throat.

"Now that's not polite." Fritz stood up, dwarfing her, and she shrank back into the nearest corner, trembling. "I asked the first question. Didn't your mother teach you it's not polite to answer a question with another question?" And he smiled broadly. Most of his menacing appearance crumbled with the expression. "I am . . ." the girl's voice cracked as she struggled to clear her throat. "I am April Adams." Tears were rolling down her cheeks now as she envisioned the giant brutally raping her.

"Well, it's nice to know I've got the right apartment." The big man walked over to an ironing board and pulled a fluffy peasant dress off it. "I represent Mr. Falconi," he said, handing the garment to her politely.

"*The* Mr. Falconi?" Her face took on a bright, surprised smile, but the Glove noticed her fingers were still shaking as she clutched the towel to her body.

"You applied for a singing role with his traveling stage performers, didn't you?" One of Glover's eyebrows jumped slightly from years of practice.

"Why yes, but so did a thousand other girls!" She turned her back to him, tied the towel around her slender waist, and pulled the dress over her head. Her reply told him she had expected the application to be promptly thrown in a trash can. "I just can't believe he—"

"He was impressed with your portfolio, miss," the hoodlum with scars crisscrossing his forehead said somberly. Black, oily bangs hid the decades-old razor wounds.

"That skinny thing?" The five-page folder flashed through her head as she zipped up the dress unaided and let the towel drop to the floor once more. "I've only had one role so far since leaving home, and that was . . ." But she hesitated. April Adams was a small town girl, but she was not totally stupid. Better not to tip her hand so soon.

"Mr. Falconi has run into some unforeseen sudden deadlines." The Glove didn't seem to hear what she had said, though in fact every word was filed away for

36

future scrutiny. "Several potential contracts have . . . dropped into his lap, so to speak. A possible opportunity for you and several other talented young women like yourself has opened up overseas. I'm sure you will be—"

"Overseas?" She whirled around excitedly, eyes sparkling, and Glover both feared and hoped she might embrace him. The tips of her breasts, still moist, pressed against the plunging neckline of the dress, and it was almost as though she were wearing nothing again. He couldn't help but think this was how his daughter had reacted when he gave her a beat-up old car for Christmas, years ago, before the courts had taken her away from him. But she had not been such a blossoming flower, and she had been wearing jeans and a T-shirt that morning so many lifetimes ago. With April Adams, the fatherly pride and refreshing memories vanished quickly enough, and all he felt for her in the end was a throbbing hardness against the inside of his pants that refused to go away.

"It's rather cold outside." Glover changed the subject and turned away from her. He opened a closet. "Best you choose some warm shoes."

"My, aren't we the authoritative one this morning." She glided past him, grinning anxiously. It never occurred to her that meeting a potential employer at five in the morning was slightly out of the ordinary. She chose a pair of black high heels, playfully ignoring his suggestion, and drew an inexpensive fur coat off a hanger. Whipping her long reddish-brown hair over a shoulder, she flashed her teeth at him and said, "Take me to you leader, big fella." The Jayne Mansfield accent was so out of place Fritz Glover winced.

Just like all the rest of 'em, he delivered judgment and the smile crumbled. *Damned models' mouth — always flashin' their choppers at every pair o' trousers that passes by. Well, Falconi'll wipe the grin off her puss soon enough.*

The stereo clicked off automatically as they approached the door.

"Everything else turned off?" Glover asked, hesitating. "The stove? The toaster?"

His sudden attention to detail both impressed and frightened April. Memories of someone in her past crept out to haunt her and she felt a chill race down her spine. Someone who was always very thorough, who had always been so precise — a perfectionist. But someone she had been too little to really know.

The stereo needle dropped against its armrest and power drained from the controls panel. "Nothing else is on," she said, opening the door for him.

As they left the dimly lit hallway and started down the outside steps, Glover motioned toward several police cars parked in front of the building. An officer could be seen teetering precariously on a ground-floor windowsill, applying fingerprint powder with a thin paintbrush.

April Adams brought her fingers up to cover her mouth. "I wonder whatever could be happening?" The question left her lips in the form of steam, rising on the brittle air.

"You should consider moving to a better neighborhood," Fritz Glover noted casually, leading her across the street to his white '64 Plymouth.

"Yes," she agreed, after a moment of silence. "The block is turning into a real slum. Perhaps Mr. Falconi is God's answer to my prayers."

Glover grinned suddenly, but he did not laugh out loud. *Don't bet on it, honey,* he responded with thoughts only as he opened the car door for her. *Don't you dare bet on it. . . .*

Angelo Falconi twisted one end of his black mustache as he inspected the young woman seated in front of his desk. The smile on his face immediately put April Adams on the defensive — her old roommate, a dancer who was now working in Vegas somewhere, had warned her about such signs — but she decided to play along for the time being. She was young, needed the exposure, and what·did she have to go back to? A crumbling tenement that rated one murder or suicide a month and a host of strong-armed robberies? She crossed her firmly toned legs and smiled back at the slender man in the three-piece suit.

Falconi's hair was combed straight back and was as dark as his mustache. Appreciating the flash of thigh, he ran his fingers through his hair and winked across the desk at April. He propped a thick notebook on the desk so that she could not see its contents. "I'm impressed with the portfolio you sent us," he said.

April knew whatever it was he held in his hands, it was not her portfolio, but she winked back and shifted her shoulders from side to side slowly, allowing one

39

side of her blouse to dip generously, revealing the top half of a breast.

"Falconi." She pronounced the three syllables slowly, making them sound like a lewd proposition. "Is that Italian?"

The man shifted about in his seat uneasily. "No." The smile remained on his face however. "It is Latin. Costa Rican, to be precise."

"*No.*" the word was spoken as if in surprise. "I don't believe it!" Her own smile brightened. Guessing nationalities had always been a challenge she enjoyed. "You're Greek, and you changed your name!"

Falconi's expression grew somewhat grim, and he checked his wrist watch. "I'm afraid we could go on with these pleasantries forever," he said politely, "but I am running late—"

"It is only quarter till six," she interrupted softly, glancing up at big, bad Glover leaning against the door, the loyal bodyguard.

"And there's a schedule to adhere to, I'm afraid."

"Of course." April lowered her head slightly in mock submission.

"You have expressed a desire to travel to faraway, exotic lands." Falconi stood up and walked over to a large map of the world covering one entire wall of his office. The room was immense, but it was lightly decorated, holding only the desk and a few chairs, and April couldn't shake the feeling this was some sort of fly-by-night operation that was here today and gone tomorrow.

She ignored her instincts again. "Yes." She joined

Falconi by the map. "The Orient has always intrigued me to no end." Big Fritz Glover focused on her shapely behind as she spoke. "And I always hoped to visit there someday."

"The Orient, eh?" Falconi took to twisting his mustache again.

"Yes, Mr. Falconi. Your advertisements stated you were looking for singers—*American* singers—to dance and perform in distant, exotic Asian ports."

"Ah, yes."

"Well, I can sing, and I can dance, and I'm even a damned good pianist, if I do say so myself."

"A pianist?"

"Yes. Didn't you get the tape I sent you?" A streak of worry creased her young brow.

"Oh, yes, yes, my dear—of course." Falconi dusted a piece of non-existent dust off the raised mountains of Burma. "And your voice sounded crystal clear—crystal clear!"

"Well, I was specifically interested in Korea. Do you have any openings in Korea?" She moved closer to him. "They call it the Land of the Morning Calm, did you know that? To me, that sounds very romantic, don't you think?"

"*Korea?*" he sounded surprised. Visions of snow and windswept guard posts came to him. "We've been sending all our girls to Tokyo recently. I don't recall hearing anything about Korea, my dear. Hell, I don't even know the capital of that godforsaken country." He glanced over at Glover inquisitively.

April Adams answered him. "Seoul," she said enthusiastically. "My father sent my mother hundreds of letters from there. He was a soldier, stationed in Korea during the war."

"I see." Falconi directed a troubled glance at the man with his back against the door.

"But he died over there." Her eyes fell to the floor. "At least that's what some of them tell me—or tried to tell me. For years they claimed he was only missing in action. Mother never listened to any of it. And now they've got her locked away in the home."

Falconi's smile returned.

"You could take your holidays in Seoul," Glover offered advice for the first time. "Japan's just a hop, skip and jump away from the ROK, young lady." He liked the way the high heels stretched her calf muscles out and tightened the lines all the way up to the contours of her hips.

"But I know my father's alive." April had appeared to drift into another world momentarily. "He's out there . . . somewhere," she said. "We might never find each other again, but at least in Korea, I'll be near the places he lived and worked, and close to the area where he disappeared."

"Wars change people and places," Glover's voice took on a melancholy tone. "It's never the same afterwards—the country. It's never the same, after war. You're wasting your time, young lady. You'd just be wasting your life over there."

Falconi did not like the direction this conversation was taking. Without April seeing the hand movement, he waved Glover out of the room, and the gentle giant left without making a sound.

"You realize, of course, that, in our business" — he draped an arm around her bare shoulder — "accommodations are not the grandest, at first. You must work your way up to that spotlight among the stars, that elusive contract for the silver screen." His nose brushed against the nape of her neck, seeking out the scent of perfume. He was pleasantly surprised to find only a clean and refreshing soapy fragrance.

"What you are trying to tell me is that I may have to work one-night gigs in some pretty seedy dives." She skillfully moved out from under his clutches without offending the man.

"You may have to do a little go-go dancing, at first," Falconi admitted.

"Yes, I anticipated I'd be spending the first couple years paying my dues, so to speak."

"So to speak." Falconi moved toward her again, pleased at how understanding she seemed.

"Will these be bars I'll be dancing in?" She brought the strap back up over her shoulder and returned to the map. "Or fancy nightclubs? I was under the impression there were no 'seedy dives' in Tokyo, Mr. Falconi."

The clever Costa Rican had glided up to his desk and was rifling through a pile of envelopes with overseas postage affixed to them and red-and-blue air mail lines along the edges. "As a matter of fact, Miss Adams —" he pulled a manila folder out from the bottom of the stack — "come to think of it — I *do* have a file here from one of our GI clubs way up on the

43

Korean DMZ. It seems they need round-eyed dough-nut dollies pretty bad up there. And the better they sing, the better the 'tips,' according to the correspondence."

"Korea?" She turned from staring up at the map to face him.

"Yes, my dear! Korea." His finger pointed to the small peninsula protruding from one edge of China.

"Oh, Mr. Falconi!" She rushed up and threw her arms around him. "You've no idea how much this means to me!"

Falconi placed his hands on her waist and pulled her close, so she could feel the bulge in his pants. "But of course this *does* involve some risk on my part," he added. "Since I *am* footing all transportation costs, connection fees and expenses, it only seems right that—"

"You are allowed to inspect the goods beforehand." She pulled loose and backed away from him slowly. Her smile was intact, but her eyes were cold as ice.

"You are very intelligent for your age, April," he said softly, folding his arms across his chest. "In this line of work, you have to make certain choices. It's time to start deciding if you want to send promo tapes to uncaring agents the rest of your life—" he stretched the facts a bit—"or if you want to latch onto this opportunity and ride it for all it's worth. Some women have gone through this world penniless because they passed up chances like this. They're still stripping past their fiftieth birthday in back-alley floorshows with their sagging tits bouncing off their pot bellies."

April tried not to picture herself in such a desperate situation, but disgusting visions flashed into her head. She maintained an emotionless expression nonetheless. "I think it's *you* who's taking this opportunity to *ride* someone, Mr. Falconi," she managed to say slyly, without being insulting. She slipped one then the other shoulder strap off, pulled down her zipper in back, and let the peasant dress fall to the floor around her ankles.

Falconi read the look on her face; it was a mixture of disgust, helplessness, and resignation. Standing before him was an inexperienced girl who felt she had no other choice at the moment. "Now you're getting the idea." He started toward her. But then he abruptly stopped as his eyes concentrated on the beauty standing unprotected and suddenly exposed in front of him. He was actually taken aback by the sight of her. The words "virgin" and . . . "sacrifice" flashed through his head.

Her breasts, firm and shapely, jutted up flawlessly at him and for some reason he thought of identical troops standing at attention, awaiting inspection. Yet at the same time he felt he was gazing upon a chest no man had ever fondled before.

Her thighs were moving back and forth slightly, nervously, as her feet shifted about in the fluffy pile of cloth. This woman was making the first truly important decision of her life, Falconi mused silently. The first vital concession. And he would be the stud to snatch away her innocence and the inner power that some believed came with such an act.

He quickly recovered, and started toward her again,

hands out at arm's length, but April took them in her own and backed away.

"No," she said firmly. "You can inspect, Mr. Falconi —" she forced an apprehensive smile —"but you cannot consume."

"But I am the boss," he replied confidently.

"Not yet," she said, allowing him to get closer, her resistance crumbling despite the reprimand.

Falconi draped his arms over her shoulders and dropped his head. He ran his tongue down her throat and across the valley below it until the swell pushed back against his lips.

With the tip of his tongue he ran circles around the nipple pulsing over her heart, but it failed to respond.

He could sense her head dropping back involuntarily — as if she were surrendering to a persistent boyfriend she nevertheless felt comfortable being with — and when a light sigh escaped her, he cupped the breast from below with his palm and pushed upward, forcing the nipple deep into his mouth until it finally shot erect. *Under duress*, the words flew through his thoughts and vanished just as quickly. *Cooperating under duress*.

His other hand slid down her rib cage and across a flat stomach to the thick mound of hair where her thighs came together.

Falconi felt her body shudder as his fingers expertly probed the folds of moist skin and entered her several inches. He sucked harder on her breast — until he could take no more flesh into his mouth, and she stepped backwards awkwardly, nearly stumbling because of the high heels.

Using the hand between her legs for leverage, he steadied her, but April's groan this time was not one of pleasure. "That's enough." The harsh whisper left her throat like a jungle cat's hiss, but her eyes were still closed.

"Have it your way." Falconi abruptly withdrew his fingers, and April stumbled again and fell to one knee on the thick carpet.

He turned his back on her as if she were not even in the room and walked back over to the huge wall map. "You sure you won't reconsider?" He paused just long enough to make her wonder which subject he was talking about.

"I really don't think—"

"Now now." He turned slightly and shook a finger at her playfully. "Let's not have any rash decisions. Tokyo can be rather pleasant this time of year—all year around in fact."

"I don't think so, Mr. Falconi." An inner sigh of relief relaxed her chest, but she said, "It will have to be Seoul, Korea, sir."

Falconi watched her clasp the peasant dress to her Ann-Margret body for a few seconds before turning to scan the tall map again. "Then Seoul it is, my dear." He resumed twisting the end of his mustache, delighting in the slight odor that suddenly assaulted his nostrils. "Seoul it is!"

"Isn't this great?" a tall, black woman in a blond wig

stared down at the tenements of north Portland as the private jet ascended up through the hazy, castlelike clouds. She watched cars racing back and forth along Lombard Street grow increasingly smaller, and sunlight sparkle off the surface of the Columbia River. "I never thought I'd get to see Macao — *all expenses paid!*"

The smiling girl seated beside her, a slender brunette wearing a plentifully stuffed black tank top and glowing white hot pants, suddenly lost the smile, and she crowded near the window — as if checking the cloud formations would tell her what direction they were travelling. "I thought we were headed for Madrid!"

"They told me Tokyo!" a Raquel Welch lookalike in tight-fitting slacks and pink sweater cast a perplexed look at the other twelve women in the craft's lounge.

"Anybody here ever hear the name Seoul, Korea?" April Adams asked softly, but her words were lost in the din of sudden commotion among the other worried passengers. She felt a cold shiver race down her back. Hesitating at first, she forced herself to her feet and walked shakily over to the unyielding partition separating the rear of the jet from the crew's quarters.

But the narrow door in the center was tightly locked from the other side.

4

Manila, Philippines

The two men following the drunk American sailor did not realize a hidden pair of eyes was in turn following *them* as they started down into the maze of dark alleys running along the riverfront off Roxas Boulevard. Monitoring their every move. Sizing them up.

So overconfident were they in "taking down" this inebriated foreigner that their cocky laughs and careless footfalls could be heard a considerable distance down either side of the block.

The sailor glanced back over one shoulder when the smaller of the two hoods knocked an empty can against the gutter. Something deep in his gut told him danger was afoot, and although his chin took to nervously bobbing up and down as he stumbled along, his eyes bulged straight ahead, unblinking, searching desperately for nothing.

The air overhead became a sudden clash of loud, chopping vibrations, and a helicopter, its lights all extinguished, passed a mere fifty yards above, unseen except as an elusive black shadow against the stars.

A jeep loaded down with militiamen cruised by through the nearest intersection, a block away and, though the driver seemed to notice the intoxicated sailor for a moment, it continued rolling down the next block—the soldiers in the back laughing boisterously at some GI joke or vulgar story.

And then the two thieves were upon the American. Moving swiftly, their smiling faces suddenly grim and businesslike, they appeared on either side of him. Each grabbed a wrist and twisted it back.

The sailor started to yell as they swung him into a dark doorway, but his face impacted against the brick wall, and he went down across the ground in a dazed heap.

The woman gliding silently through the shadows appeared behind the Filipinos as they were bending over, going through their victim's pockets.

Amy Atencio, her slender, finely toned body nearly invisible against the night because of her black coveralls, drew the sleek commando knife from a calf sheath and plunged it down through the top of the larger man's skull.

The blade crashed out his mouth in a bloody spray, severing his tongue, silencing his startled cry and breaking off several teeth in front.

She encountered a problem withdrawing the weapon from the tough, layered bone—no matter how hard she jerked on it—and as the robber's partner whirled around, pistol in hand, she kicked him aggressively, in a blinding, martial-arts prance, tearing into his groin and lower abdomen. Amy grabbed his hands as he flopped to the ground, groaning.

Imminent death inspires latent reserves of strength, regardless of the injuries or pain someone is enduring, and the hood resisted. They began wrestling across the blacktop, struggling for the revolver.

But Amy's adrenaline had been racing through her system longer — her fighter's body, which went through a rigorous routine of offensive jui-jitsu exercises every morning at dawn, was charged with energy. In seconds, she had the revolver twisted around, the barrel forced into the thief's belly.

And the gun barked once. Wiping the man's expression blank, the slate clean. Smoke floated up from their tangled arms, filling her nostrils. A licoricelike taste coated her throat instantly, and she flashed back for a moment to the endless days spent at the LZ London firing range in Colorado — so many lifetimes ago, it seemed — when Ross had first taken her under his wing. *Wings of a bloodthirsty condor,* she thought to herself, the sentence hanging bitterly in her mind, refusing to fall apart, floating away on the polluted river of black memories, down to the Dead Sea of hate.

A sedan roared through an empty intersection blocks down the hill. Sparks shot out from its undercarriage as it bounced off a dip in the road. It was closely followed by a speeding police car, red-and-blue roof lights twirling furiously. The high-low siren brought Amy back to reality from the surrealistic slow-motion blur of gunfighting and violent death. But the autos were gone just as quickly as they had appeared. The siren's echo bounced back and forth off several high tenement buildings, grew suddenly louder, then faded altogether. Amy watched the glowing sparks in the distant intersection fizzle out.

A huge tomcat raced up to one unusually large piece of smoking body metal, and battered it about with its paw.

Amy glanced around. The hot, muggy air seemed unusually cool, her vision extraordinarily clear and sharp, but she knew it was just the adrenaline rush reaching a peak.

Nobody appeared to be watching her, but she could feel the countless sets of eyes peering down at her from the shuttered windows looking out over the alley.

Amy, her chest still gasping in lungfuls of the moist, sticky air, glanced down at the men lying at her feet — their still forms half visible just beyond the outline of her heaving breasts.

She bent over slightly, slipped her blood-caked knife back in its velcro sheath, then placed her boot under one of the dead Filipinos and pushed him over onto his stomach. The wallet was sticking half out of a back pocket.

She pulled it out, removed the money — about twenty dollars' worth of local currency — and glanced through the photo section. It was empty except for a couple of X-rated poses clipped from some European porno magazine.

The woman with her hair drawn back in a black ponytail tossed the wallet into the stagnant canal at the edge of the blacktop and commenced removing the dead man's jewelry: a heavy gold necklace, two cast-silver rings and a cheap wrist watch. She went through his pockets quickly, then repeated the procedure on the second corpse, though he carried no wallet.

"How ya doin', honey?" She gently grabbed a handful of the sailor's bushy hair and lifted his face out of the trash piled in the doorway.

Amy's stomach bellyflopped, but she kept the queasy feeling confined to her gut. The American's face had been slammed into the brick wall so violently the splinterlike bones inside his nose had been forced up into the brain. One massive bump had risen between his eyes, the blood was everywhere.

He was as dead as the others.

Amy released his hair, letting his head flop back into the paper sacks and discarded fruit. She shrugged her shoulders for her own benefit—her own sanity—and patted him down swiftly, checking for valuables. They would do the sailor no good now.

"Poor baby-san," she whispered to the dead American serviceman. "So young. Haven't even been around long enough to lose your cherry, right, honey? How many Filipino hearts have you managed to break during your short career with the United States Naval establishment? Does a young girl wait for you at this very moment to come home to her loving embrace? Some illiterate peasant girl willing to surrender everything to you in hopes you will reward her dedication with a wedding band and that precious airplane ticket back to the Big PX?" Hearing her sarcasm-soaked words made Amy hesitate continuing her conversation with the round-eyed corpse, and the ominous silence that followed saddened her deeply. She wanted to cry—not because of the terrible fate that had befallen the sailor, or even the hoods at her feet. But because, partially, of what her simple life had—or had not— amounted to, and more important, because she still possessed that splinter of sanity that separated her from the other killers roaming the dark back alleys of the Orient.

Amy felt that, so long as she realized exactly what she was doing—who she was murdering and why she was doing it—and could remember the acts afterwards, she had not tripped off that dangerous edge that separated her from the madmen of the earth. There was no forgetting the deeds that had brought her to this point in her travels—Manila—but so long as she could rationalize the acts she had committed, this female war dog would be able to maintain her sanity.

Female war dog. The thought, the words made her smile despite all that had happened in the last five minutes. *More like battle bitch!*

Headlights suddenly bathed the alleyway in brilliant silver, as an American Air Force SP jeep on routine patrol appeared, but Amy Atencio had vanished—a shadow in the night.

Somewhere along the Vietnamese-Cambodian border

Ex-mercenary and one-time paratrooper over the skies of Korea, Chad Chandler, took another swallow from the pigskin flask of rice wine and hugged the woman lying against his chest with his free arm. They both gazed up at the sparkling stars hanging motionless above a rare break in the triple canopy of rain forest. Now and then sparks from the dozen campfires encircling them took to the warm breeze and swirled upward, toward the break in the branches.

"We call them forest furies," the Khmer woman—*his woman*—explained in mixed Cambodian and pidgin

English as she pointed up at the glowing embers. "They are *bookoo* good luck, Chad. They keep back the jungle spirits. They keep us safe at night."

"They are nothing more than dying puffs of smoke." Chandler acted amused as the slurred words left him. "*I* am that which protects you from the jungle spirits, Zemm."

In the background, Khmer men made primitive music with dozens of native drums, and maidens in loose sarongs that stopped at the waist danced about, entertaining them.

A child cried, somewhere in one of the longhouses that extended for a hundred yards below the huge palace built into the cliff. "I must attend to your son." Zemm moved to rise, but Chandler held her tight.

"You will spoil him." Chandler's eyes were still on the stars. "Let the girl attend to his needs. Relax, for a change."

"Her breasts are not with milk," she argued mildly, gazing up at the galaxies now too. "The boy wants mine, or else he will cry through the night — don't you men understand that?" She twisted his belly skin slightly, though it was mostly flat muscle and hard to grasp. "Infants can tell a stranger's nipple, unlike you soldiers — who will settle for any mouthful!"

She was going to slap him lightly, like she always did when they lay by the campfires at night and she inevitably brought up the subject of other women. But then the star appeared again, and the sight of its golden glow made her silent.

"There it is." Chandler checked his wristwatch. "Right on time."

"I still can not believe it is made by your people,"

55

Zemm's eyes refrained from blinking now, and her lips parted slightly in awe as she followed the satellite across the heavens.

"Have I ever lied to you before?" Chandler's hand slid in under her blouse and caressed a breast. His tone taunted her for a mischievous reply, but before she could speak he had brushed the fabric aside and pressed his lips against the soft, brown whirl, now rapidly growing taut.

Her heart beating furiously, Zemm cupped his head in her hands and let her own fall back into the soft pile of blankets. Sometimes his lips treated her to the most shocking surprises—sometimes his tongue slid all the way down her body, but that was only inside the hut, when they were alone, and now there were so many of her people in sight, though most of them were stumbling about in a drunken stupor and probably wouldn't notice if they took to abandoning their clothes and thrashed about in the elephant grass at the edge of the woods. Zemm found herself hoping her man would surprise her with a little bit of daring tonight.

"Have you ever lied to me before?" she repeated his earlier question because it seemed suddenly, stupidly proper, and her eyes opened just in time to watch the satellite vanish beyond the tangle of tree limbs above. "Only if I count the time I caught you with that child beneath the last longhouse."

"She's sixteen, minimum," Chad said confidently, careful to keep her subdued with his lips.

"She was a sixteen-year-old *child*!" There was no anger in her tone.

"She is still a virgin," he added.

"Only because I caught you in time!" She slapped

56

the back of his head lightly, then caressed it, keeping it down as his lips moved in tight circular motions along the bottom of her rib cage. "A minute more and you would have two sons to provide for!"

"And two wives!" Chandler took flesh between his teeth and nibbled on it, but did not bite her.

"Ha!" she replied defiantly. "You think so, my dear husband?"

"I am not yet your husband, my dear Zemm," he matched her grim humor.

"You are the father of our son!" She grabbed a handful of hair, threatening to pull it out if his direction of conversation did not abruptly change.

"Perhaps I am the father of many sons, my dear— did you ever think of that? Perhaps I have a son in every port: Hong Kong, Singapore, Tokyo, Seoul. . . ."

"I have never heard of these places, so you must be making them up," she half kidded him, though her eyes were beginning to grow moist, tiring of the game.

"You have heard Princess Raina talk of our bravery," Chandler decided to see how far he could go. "Of our daring and—"

"Surely she would not exaggerate." Zemm made her smile return as she spoke sarcastically yet reverently in a double-tongued reply.

"You have seen her try and make Justin head of her Palace Guard—"

"Yet he would have nothing of such nonsense!" she lashed back at him.

"Nonsense?" Chandler cast her a look that said, mockingly, *You could lose your head over a remark like that.*

"You know what I mean. You men are foreign

born. Why would you want to spend the rest of your lives in this jungle when you could return to — to — The World?" She glanced away in pain.

Chandler's own eyes took on a faraway, peaceful look that told the woman perhaps he had found his private, little slice of paradise in this restless rain forest, with this hidden, little hamlet, deep in its heart. "You talk like that, yet you admit I am the father of your son. *You* allow me to remain under your roof, Zemm!" His eyes narrowed, almost suspiciously, but the expression was a mask — inside, he was laughing at the conversation. He had gone through it all before, in some manner or other, with some woman or other, in some port or other. Now his life had evolved to a point where he just refused to take any of it seriously. Family or friends. In the end, what did it all matter? One child, none, or a thousand — who really cared except the bastards themselves, once their mothers kicked them out of the hut. It made no matter to him. Chandler had seen too many men die of ulcers and related illnesses after spending their lives and their resources worrying about their mistakes. He just didn't care anymore. He loved Zemm — he truly believed that. And he felt an inner glow whenever he walked into a room and saw his son on the blanket, staring back at him, wide-eyed. But he refused to lose sleep over the gnawing feelings in his gut. Perhaps if he were a Khmer soldier, committed to defending the clearing, and the border, and the stone palace, things would be different. But Chad Chandler was a different kind of soldier. His destiny took him to the other side of the world — his missions always sent him beyond dusk's last horizons. The sun never rose for him, unless he was chasing it from above the clouds, high above the earth, in a paratrooper plane, his chute harness the only breast that mothered him or offered comfort. Otherwise, he slept through the dawns.

Tonight, he leaned back on his elbows and gazed up at the stars again, suddenly ignoring Zemm. The act in itself was a mere tease, but instead of jabbing him in the side like she usually did, the Cambodian woman seemed to melt against his solid frame, taking a supportive shape beside him as she too watched the satellite disappear. "Sometimes I think I never want to leave this place." He finally admitted something she had suspected all along. "Sometimes I think maybe I want to pack you up and the little one too and just hide from Ross and the others until they go and then just live the rest of my life out here — with your people. It would make everything so simple."

"But other times . . ." She led him into the usual argument, biting her lip as she did it — mentally reprimanding herself at the same time.

"Other times I realize my place is on the battlefield with Ross and the others. Besides — "

"He would hunt you down to the death if you ever deserted him." She was rapidly tiring of the same old sentences.

"But it is nice to stare up at the stars and dream," he admitted, sighing deeply. Zemm held him tightly, and he felt her body, in turn, shudder slightly.

She stared up at a particular constellation on the edge of the galaxy, trying to remember what Chad had named it — a bear, or something — whatever a bear was. And she remembered all the evenings they had lain here before the child came, and how, sometimes, they talked for hours, until the gold star passed overhead several times. And she still couldn't believe it was thrown into the night by men raised in her man's homeland.

"When will they be back?" She spoke the words like the mere mention of "them" would open a· Pandora's box of evil and ill fortune.

"They?" Chandler still had that far-off look in his eyes—they seemed dazed. *Coated with stardust,* Zemm decided silently, growing angry with his ability to drift away from her so easily, mentally, when he held her in his arms physically.

"They!" She shot the word back at him like an arrow, but it ricocheted harmlessly like flint against steel. "Justin and the others!"

"They have taken a hop to Manila, my dear." He ran his lips along the nape of her neck, breathing in the fragrance of her long, clean hair. It felt like silk against his skin, and this time she did not brush him away. "They could be gone for years. *Decades!*" he laughed hopefully.

"And what about the upcoming mission?" The starlight reflected cruelly in her sad eyes as they stared at each other for the first time in hours.

"Mission?" Chandler feigned total surprise, but there was no shock in the words. "What mission?"

"It is all over the camp," she answered matter-of-factly. "Everyone knows your team will be leaving us soon. To go back over the mountain and kill somebody in Viet Nam. So don't lie to me, husband."

Big Chad ignored the last word in her statement, but cocked his head at her suspiciously instead. The ruthless grin remained intact. "And from whom did

60

you learn about this alleged mission, my dear?"

Zemm glanced up at the black sky in time to see a falling star shoot across the break in the dense canopy. "From the old mama-san who does the laundry at Justin's longhouse," she revealed proudly, hoping he was impressed with her intelligence sources. "She learns about anything that is brewing in the camp, eventually, and could not keep a secret if her life depended on it."

"It very well could." He flashed teeth down at her while his mind envisioned a machete lopping off the old woman's startled head from behind. "But talk is cheap, my beloved." He spoke the last word as if reading from a play without sincerity. "And I suggest you don't listen to it. I know nothing more than you do, apparently. Our little friend, Miss Atencio, has got her tit in a wringer out Manila-way, and after Ross rips it out and drags her young ass back to Indochina, we'll take it all from there. One step at a time. Sure, Roscoe received some kind of Dick Tracy message that we were to embark on another undercover mission of some sort, but until he makes me start up on the push-ups again and passes out the camo-cosmetics, I'm not going to worry about it a whole lot, OK?" He ran his hand down along her side, stopped at the swell of her hip, and slid inward until he had reached the trees at the edge of the forest. "So why don't we just kick back and enjoy ourselves in the meantime, baby-san."

Zemm grabbed his wrist, preventing his fingers from probing any further, but her smile — though tight around the edges — was still intact. "Yea, though I walk through the valley of the shadow of death —"

"I shall fear no evil —"

61

"For I am the—"

Big Chad's smile blossomed into an evil death's-head grin. *"Meanest motherfucker in the valley!"*

She released his wrist, and they rolled into the nearby reeds until they were hidden from the others at the closest campfire. Pulling her sarong away, he spread her legs apart with a knee and lowered himself onto her. Zemm arced her back upward and thrust her breasts at him, and when he entered her, plunging to his full length with the first stroke, her cry was lost in the clamor of beating drums and dancing maidens.

Manila, Philippines

Amy glanced back over her shoulder several times, but as she left the dark otherworld of the back alleys and entered the brightly lit neon boulevard down the block from her hotel, she failed to detect anyone following her.

She crossed Rizal Park, then P. Burgos Street, and entered the Manila Hotel through a rear door, reaching her room on the second floor without encountering any other guests.

She fumbled with the key at first, then mentally reprimanded herself for letting the incident trouble her—it was no different from the countless other killings she had been involved in since being "drafted" into Justin Ross's war dogs. But then she noticed the crimson stains in the middle of the black boot toe, and the sight sent her fingers to shaking again. The key ring clattered atop the hard teakwood floor.

"Christ, Amy!" she muttered another self-rebuke under her breath as she bent over to recover the keys.

A loud wolf whistle somewhere to the rear filled the narrow corridor, and Amy's eyeballs rolled toward the ceiling in resignation. *What else could go wrong?* How many more men would she have to dust before she could get a decent night's sleep? Flaring thighs tensed and visible even beneath the harsh fabric of her pants, Amy straightened up, assuming a catlike defensive stance.

She turned slowly to lock eyes with another American sailor, but the tall, lanky Hispanic was not alone. A Filipino prostitute clung to his arm like luggage, and she avoided Amy's gaze but made a special effort to swish her hips at the woman in black as they passed.

"Hey, mama, where you been keepin' yo' self all this poor sailorman's life?" he asked in a flirtatious tone, but the girl on his arm grabbed a handful of his haunches and took immediate control, guiding him on down the hallway and around a corner before Any could answer with a much-practiced comeback insult.

"Say, mama!" The sailor directed his words at his "date" now. "You sure not very sociable this evening, now, are ya?" And he chuckled. "But I guess I's can understand, you're anxious to spread 'em wide open for *papa!*"

The American's jive accent made Amy angry and suddenly in the mood for conflict, but the couple was gone that quick. A door slammed somewhere out of sight, and the only noise remaining was traffic sounds filtering through a shuttered window at the end of the hallway, from the crowded street below.

Amy smiled as she retrieved the keys and tried again. It had been so easy for just once in her life to bite her lip, control her reflexes and spare the man's life.

She would have to try that approach a little more often in the future.

After closing the door behind her, Amy walked directly to the bed and sat down on its edge, mentally exhausted. Her muscles relaxed, her body fell limp. Her fingers uncoiled, and the hotel keys fell to the floor again.

The room imitated her inner silence. For a moment.

Then a creaking on the other side of the wall broke the spell: mattress springs.

And above the ceiling. In the room directly overhead, upstairs. More bouncing springs. Another boom-boom girl earning her bucks.

The growing chorus of sounds mushroomed into a dull crescendo as a door slammed next door and more occupants went straight for the mattress to test it out. Amy laughed loudly and fell back on her own bed — she had moved into a bordello, it seemed!

She spent several seconds staring up at the ceiling fan, twirling lazily directly over her face. She felt no breeze — it only seemed to be pushing the stagnant layers of heat about so they could be replaced by an oppressive mugginess creeping in through the shutters of the window. A tiny lizard, clinging upside-down to a corner of the ceiling, screamed reptilian obscenities down at her, then abruptly fell silent, and she closed her eyes, willing the forces of sleep to close in on her.

Something fell from the bed onto the floor — something soft, padded. And out of habit she sat up, chasing away the fatigue, and glanced down at her feet.

One of the dead men's wallets had fallen from her

pocket. She started to reach down to pick it up but hesitated, then fell backward onto the bed again. It was going nowhere. And she was rapidly running out of stamina to retrieve anything — sanity, self-preservation, self-respect, self-esteem — let alone a lousy wallet.

It was the American's.

And try as she would, sleep and the sedative of exhaustion escaped her. Instead, her head filled with visions of the dead sailor and the men who had killed him. And who she had then killed.

She felt no remorse.

She was alone in the big city on an island paradise that was also home to communist insurgency warfare, a high crime rate and spreading anti-American sentiment. Someone had broken into her hotel room her first week in Manila, stealing her money, passport and possessions. The embassy would have turned her away, had she gone there for help, but Ross had taught her better.

American embassies overseas might be a haven of safety for U.S. tourists, but not for Ross's people. They were taught to keep a low profile when in between missions. And while on an op, they were virtually invisible.

Allowing herself to be victimized by a lowlife burglar in the first place was insulting enough, but to cable Ross for help was the ultimate agony.

What was done was done. Until the war dogs arrived, if they even chose to, it was up to Amy herself to survive her situation and provide the daily meal ticket. The silver she kept in an ankle bag would run out at the end of the week, and then she would be out on the street.

The streets.

The thought made her smile despite the depressing situation she found herself in. The street was her turf. The street she knew and understood. The street was where, all things considered, she really felt at home. Ross and his boys had let her grow soft these last several months—never mind all the hard-core training. And now it was time to slam a board on the bogeyman's nose. Put a stop to it all—the terror of suddenly being alone. Helpless, without the team to back you up.

And that was why the two men had had to die in a back alley beside the water's edge. And why she felt nothing about plunging home the blade.

Amy placed her hands against her hips and pressed hard. Still smooth and shapely. She ran her fingers up along her sides, then over her breasts, rubbing in tight, tender circles until her nipples grew hard.

She slipped her left forefinger into the zipper ring under her throat, and drew it down to her abdomen, opening the one-piece coveralls across the chest.

Now she could feel the downdraft from the ceiling fan.

With her right hand she lightly brushed the nipples back and forth until they stretched to their fullest. The other slid down across her flat stomach into the bushy mound, and as she pressed downward with it, she thought of Brent, and how it felt to have him on top of her . . . his weight moving in rhythm with hers, against hers, with hers.

There came a sudden knock at the door and it was like rolling a grenade under her bed. Amy sat up, jerked the zipper tight, and glided across the floor.

Her eye pressed against the peephole at the same time her lips parted, but she did not ask who it was—she recognized Ross and the two men behind him instantly.

Amy threw the door open and, unable to control herself, held her arms out to the unsmiling Army lieutenant, but no sooner had she called his name then a powerful blast down on the ground floor shook the hotel and the lights dimmed, flickered, then went out altogether.

5

Bits of plaster and spirals of dust fell from the ceiling as the hotel walls shuddered again. Ross leaped through the doorway, grabbed Amy's arm and pulled her toward the bed.

As if they'd practiced it a hundred times before, the two slid under the frame and pulled the mattress down across the side nearest the door. Collins and Sewell each chose opposite corners of the room and took up seated cross-legged positions there, with their arms folded over heads that were cradled in laps.

A ceiling beam of thick iron groaned and collapsed, and one end fell across the bed's headboard, shattering it into tiny splinters with a deafening crash. An instant later the building fell silent and there were no secondary explosions.

"Everyone alright?" Ross's voice boomed across the dark room. He knew Amy was unharmed, Her chest, panting and firm, was against his. He realized a part of the ceiling had collapsed and his thoughts were with Collins and Sewell. He felt no arousal—her perfume irritated him, in fact. His only concern was for his "other" men.

"Yeah, I'm OK." An unconfident Sewell brushed dust off his shirt.

"What the hell happened?" Collins sounded bothered by the unexpected explosion.

The Nam this wasn't!

Ross was equally irritated. "Some kind of disturbance down in the street, I would wager," he said.

"Youz dudes sure blew into town with a bang." Amy placed both hands against Justin's chest and pushed herself away from him.

"Very funny." Sewell's tone said he was totally unaroused as he watched the well-proportioned Guatemalan roll to her knees and slowly rise to her feet, her balance seemingly hampered for a hanging second by the obvious weight of her chest. Amy was tall—five-seven or eight, but she was not top-heavy. Everything fit together perfectly, so far as Brent Collins, her old hammock-chum was concerned.

Amy turned to Ross. "Youz clowns didn't piss off some cabbie downstairs or something, did ya?" Her eyes had a serious cast to them, but whenever her jaw moved about like it was chewing gum—and her mouth was actually empty, like now—they all knew she was just mocking them.

"The smartest thing to do in a situation like this," Ross decided, ignoring her remark, "would be to trot on downstairs and investigate."

"I ain't goin' back down there!" Sewell feigned intense concern for his personal safety.

"It's just them damn commie Moslems from down in Mindanao causin' trouble, Justin. It don't concern us none, OK? They probably just rolled a grenade into a police kiosk or something."

69

"Let's go." Ross started for the door, and they all followed him without further protest.

The corridor was crowded with other hotel guests rushing about like cattle sent into a frenzy by a sudden lightning storm. Outside the window, distant sirens were slowly growing louder. In the street below, several horns were honking.

When they finally reached the ground floor, Ross and the others quickly saw the reason for discontent among the many disgruntled drivers: a brightly decorated jeepney lay on its side across half the roadway, burning furiously. Some terrorist had gone and blocked their path by blowing up an unattended vehicle.

As the Americans pressed wary faces against lobby windows outside the hotel restaurant, the jeepney's gas tank ruptured and exploded. The rising fireball illuminated their curious expressions for a second, then a wall of dense smoke rolled out against the buildings rising up around the burning vehicle, obscuring everything.

"Hope the dude had insurance," Sewell remarked sarcastically as the four of them turned and walked into the restaurant.

"It wasn't *your* transportation?" Amy locked eyes with Ross, relieved. "That mess out there isn't connected with *you* guys at all?"

"Never saw the thing before," Collins answered for him. His face was an emotionless mask. "We *jogged* on down here from Clark."

Amy shot him a skeptical glance, then caught herself as her eyes began to drop to his crotch out of habit. Blushing, she turned away just as a dark-complected hostess appeared, directing them to a large table against the far wall. Dressed in unflattering black tunic and trousers, the woman's hair was longer than Amy's but rolled into a bun and balanced on top of her head with pins. Her body was slender and, to Collins, "starved." Like she needed a real man to fill her up, to *satisfy her.* She stared at Amy, ignoring the men for the most part, and as her eyes critically inspected Miss Atencio from head to toe in the space of a split-second, Ross and Sewell exchanged humored winks. The way women sized each other up on the street was always funny to the war dogs, especially when they were in Asia and it involved Amy. If looks could kill, the beautiful assassin would already have died a thousand deaths. A woman's silent appraisal of another female — always done with a frowning scowl when she thinks no one else is watching — was often more than enough to put two boxers squaring up in the ring to shame.

"Give us a few minutes to decide," Ross said in precise *Pilipino,* picking up a menu though he had no intention of ordering anything.

"So tell us what trouble you've gotten your pretty, young ass into this time." Sewell grinned across the table after the hostess left.

"It's a long story." Amy rubbed her upper arms and shivered, staring down at the plate in front of her.

"We've got all night." Ross sounded patient but noncommittal.

"And it better be good." Collins prayed it somehow involved sex. After all, she *had* come all the way over here looking for "a good time." Latin lovers that could not be found in Cambodia were rumored to be a dime a dozen in the Philippines.

Amy told them about her uneventful first week in Manila. And about the handsome political activist she had met at a downtown park shortly thereafter. The man spent his long nights wooing her—or so she claimed, while staring unwaveringly across the table at Brent—and his days behind a bullhorn, badmouthing U.S. "intervention" in Indochina and protesting his own president's "poor civil rights record" and dictatorial ways. She finally tired of his poor performance in the sack and his anti-government rhetoric, and set about investigating the possibility of gathering evidence on his activities to present to the Filipino authorities.

"The lousy dude wasn't the lonely bachelor he made himself out to be, either," she explained, the expected frown missing from her blank expression. "Seems he has two or three wives spread around throughout the islands. And five daughters practically out of their teens."

"Five." Collins held the fingers of one hand up in front of Sewell's face. The look in his eyes told the chopper pilot, *Now that's a challenge!*

Amy's own brow narrowed, signalling her irritation at the interruption, and Brent shrugged his shoulders in mock embarrassment like a schoolboy who had just been caught cheating on a test. "And damned if all five of them didn't start shadowing me, Justin. Everywhere I went! I still don't know if they just felt they had to look out for their old man, or if they're employed by the government, for Christsake—but it became a real pain in the ass *real quick*. I even suspect they were behind the break-in last week. All my valuables, goddamnit! Everything! The little cunts got it all."

Collins broke into another ear-to-ear grin. "I love that kind of talk!" His head bobbed about in no apparent direction until it came to rest staring at Matt.

"And I thought we taught you better," Sewell replied to Amy's story.

"Why the hell did you leave your passport and everything in the hotel room, anyway?" the lieutenant agreed with Sewell.

"You don't understand." Amy stood up and angrily flexed her chest at them. Sewell and Collins both put on their best drooling display, but she ignored them. "I really wanted to get this bastard bad, Roscoe."

"Real righteous." Her team leader did not sound all that sincere. "But—"

"And to really get him with his pants down—" she stepped in between Ross and the other two men, turning her back to Collins and Sewell.

"This is getting juicy," Sewell whispered over to the ex-policeman loud enough for Amy to hear.

"To really get him with the goods," Amy continued, "to where he'd really open up to me, I knew I'd have to drop my own drawers at his pad." Ross, already looking down on her, cast Amy a disapproving smirk. "How else was I to take him into my confidence?" Anger flared in her own narrowed eyes.

"Lovers stupidly tell everything to one another in the heat of passion," Sewell unexpectedly came to her defense, though the glare Amy threw him said his words were unwelcomed.

"And it just so happens the unknown cat burglars struck on the same night you were being so dedicated to your duty," Collins stated cruelly.

Ross did not give her a chance to lash out at him. "Did it work?" he asked matter-of-factly.

Amy hesitated for a moment, and her eyes fell to the floor as she seemed to contemplate her answer. Outside, the sound of several boots walking down the hallway could suddenly be heard. "You don't understand what I went through before I fled Guatemala as a girl." Her eyes grew moist, but she refused to cry. "The communists from the countryside were horrible —"

"You had commie problems way back then?" Collins sounded skeptical. "Down in that part of Central America?" He was in the mood to argue.

Amy was not about to dignify their status by using a political label. "They were terrorists!" She looked up at Brent finally. Her eyes burned into him. "Plain and simple. I will never forget them. And I will never forgive —"

"OK, alright." Collins backed off, his hands raised in surrender.

"In this bastard I saw the opportunity to strike a private, little blow at the Red Menace machine here in Southeast Asia —"

"Isn't that what we've been doing for the last year?" Ross asked, but Amy's eyes were locked on Brent's.

A private little blow, Sewell thought to himself, smiling inwardly, not impressed with the patriotic speech. But he fought off the impulse to make a wisecrack and instead remained silent.

"You didn't answer my question," Ross said. "Did it work, my dear?" The affectionate title sounded like it came more from an elderly man to his infant granddaughter than from sarcastic officer to embarrassed soldier.

But Amy did not have time to answer.

A loud smash against the other side of the door sent the four of them whirling to face it. The wood held, though it creaked, shuddered and nearly splintered under the heavy impact, and before the team could react, a second set of shoulders crashed into it and the frame collapsed inward, revealing a squad of soldiers and several policemen standing out in the hallway.

Submachine guns bristling at the ready, a dozen Filipinos rushed into the small hotel room.

Though they were all armed, either with commando knives in calf sheaths or automatics in shoulder holsters, the war dogs' hands slowly went up above their heads, offering no resistance.

6

Army Lt. Justin Ross could tell by the expression on the military commander's face that nothing he could say right now would do any good—the Filipinos meant business. And they looked angry, which meant, for some reason, they were taking all this personally—it was not just another after-dark hotel raid.

But Ross spoke anyway. "I believe you gentlemen have the wrong room." A slight smile erupted across his usually grim features. "If you'll listen carefully, you can still hear the bedsprings bouncing like crazy *next door*. The whores are having their party one room over, fellas."

The tall, stocky soldier with the mahogany face and captain's insignia on his collar didn't even bother to look at Ross. His boiling eyes drilled into Amy's. "Your name, miss." He reached into his thigh pocket and pulled out a small plastic bag with a re-sealable top. Before Amy could reply, the captain slipped a passport from the clear container. "Your name is

Candice Marsh?"

Amy inwardly winced but her face remained expressionless. She hated the cover name. Especially since the men always shortened it to Candy and teased her about how their hungry tongues longed to lick Candy's cane. Amy nodded slightly in the affirmative.

The captain turned to one of his subordinates and spoke rapidly in *Pilipino*. The soldier in turn shouted something down the hallway, and moments later two militiamen appeared in the doorway with a young woman between them. She was no prisoner, but looked more like a witness to something.

Amy immediately recognized her as one of the daughters of the radical she had been trying to frame. Her body tingled for a second or two, then the feeling went away, but she knew deep in her gut that the tables were being turned against her.

Brent Collins sensed. what they were up to also. "We've been up here in this room for the last hour," he exaggerated, but nobody was listening anyway.

The woman's arm shot out and she pointed directly at Amy before unleashing a torrent of frightened accusations. When she ended her sentence, the captain rushed forward and slapped a set of handcuffs across Amy's wrist, so hard in fact the bone nearly cracked in protest.

"She claims she saw you plant the bomb near the open-air restaurant downstairs that has killed dozens of Filipinos!" he said, as fire truck sirens and ambulances could be heard pulling up to the scene outside. Ross wondered why he even bothered to explain the charges. "We have four more people waiting below who also claim to have seen you commit the act." His face

77

displayed no satisfaction at making the arrest, but only horror over the savagery of the bombing.

"Four Filipino women?" Amy's own expression took on resigned lines of hopelessness.

"Yes." The captain grabbed her arm after she was handcuffed behind the back and hustled her toward the door.

Amy glanced back at Ross and Collins before she disappeared out into the hallway. Her eyes told the two men she realized it was better if they took no action then and there. "Four women," she muttered under her breath, loud enough for the American lieutenant to hear. "I should have known."

"Korea it isn't." April Adams's fingers tore through the damp tissue her hands had been wringing the last two or three thousand air miles. Below, the shimmering turquoise-blue of the deceptively calm sea was giving way to stepping-stone shades of lush green as a wall of impenetrable jungle signalled land, and rice paddies rose up through the hostile mountain valleys.

"That's not Japan down there." More girls were crowding around the tiny aircraft windows to gaze down through the floating fortresses of clouds.

"I been to Japan once before," another potential starlet declared. "And that ain't Japan, honey! Where's all the buildings?"

Snow should be blanketing the ground, April thought to herself as the wing flaps fell slightly and the plane began its descent. *This time of year, snow should be one long sheet of white down there. Instead, it looks like the* National Geographic *pictures of the Amazon.*

"I'm tellin' you all," still another of the beautiful dancers voiced her uneasy opinion. "We are headed for *Spain*! They promised me Madrid."

The girl who had been to Japan before laughed loudly, though her voice too was tainted with uncertainty. "That ain't *Spain* down there, honey." Her smile faded as their eyes met. "I guarantee it."

Wisps of cumulus fogged up the windows as the craft descended through the gauze of clouds, and then they were drifting only a few thousand feet above the treetops of the restless rain forest.

Now and then narrow roads crisscrossed the green maze. They always seemed clogged with trucks, and water buffalos being led by bent-over old men could even be seen through some breaks in the dense foliage. The old men often wore strange-looking, straw conical hats. April thought they looked too skinny and frail to be Koreans.

Atop one of the cumbersome animals, several naked children ran back and forth across its back, engaging in juvenile horseplay. Others frolicked in the muddy canals along the side of the road. The water buffalos continued to walk along, unbothered and unimpressed, their jaws munching feed, their tails swishing at clouds of mosquitoes not visible from the air. One of the agile children pushed another off the water buffalo's back, and he plunged into the stagnant canal, only to surface a second later, grinning impishly, but the scene failed to bring the smile to April's own lips it normally would have. She wondered if, sometime during the night, she had crossed over into the dark world of her nightmares and left reality far behind. She began worrying about what awaited her on the ground—and if they would even make it down there: heavy turbulence was trying to pull the craft apart, it seemed, and as it bucked and bounced on the rough air waves, the ominous jungle below began looking more and more like menacing jaws of death, waiting restlessly to swallow the tiny plane up.

"Over there! Look over there!" The girl who thought they were going to Macao pointed out one of the windows on the other side of the craft, and the women, like a mindless school of fish, flocked over beside her. All except April, who felt suddenly too weak to move.

Two gunships could be seen halfway down between the plane and the ground and approximately a thousand feet distant, maneuvering around a stretch of clearing in opposing circles. Showering the grid of land with automatic tracer fire, the pilots of each helicopter tightened the size of the kill zone with each successive pass.

"Are they shooting guns?" asked the black girl with the blond wig, her long, slender fingers held across bright red lips.

"Well, what the hell does it look like, stupid?" A chesty broad from Texas thrust her breasts at her, careful to keep her nose in the air. "I guarantee you they ain't huntin' coons with old socks down there!"

"Well, I just never saw such . . . rods of light like that before. It looked so . . . beautiful." She continued staring down at the escalating firefight. Now and then a green tracer arced up at the choppers from the trees, contrasting sharply with the rain of red dropping from the gunships. "What in the Lord's name could they be shooting at?" She either didn't detect the hostility in the blonde's tone or was ignoring it completely.

"I'd venture a guess we're landing in a war zone somewhere, deary." A slender Latino consulted her makeup mirror and began applying a crimson shade of lipstick. "I just hope they got a postcard rack at the airport."

"I just hope they got an airport!" The blonde laughed nervously.

"A war zone?" another up-and-coming starlet spoke in a dumb blonde accent as she glanced over at the streetwise Texan. "Are we at war with anybody these days?"

"There's no rules statin' we gotta get shanghaied to a country the U.S. is fightin'," the Latino answered for her. "On any given day anywhere across the globe there's a couple dozen splendid little wars going on, baby."

"Any of you rocket scientists ever hear of Viet Nam?" The Texan stared across the seats at April, who remained frozen while heads on the other women bobbed back and forth ignorantly.

"Viet *what*?" The black woman cocked her head to one side.

"Jesus." The Texan came across suddenly annoyed at having to explain everything. "They really turn out some dumb sambos down on the plantation these days, don't they." And she turned away to face the other girls. "I got a brother in the Army. He's in charge of one of them river boats down in the Delta. He says—"

"Why, you *bitch*!" The insult registered on the black dancer with a delayed reaction. She suddenly charged across the aisle and slammed into the beauty queen from Dallas, fists raised. Both women bounced off the wall and over the seat into the laps of two other girls and all four began clawing each other and pulling out hair. Dresses ripped down the middle, halter tops were torn open and tight hot pants popped at the seams. Curses and screams filled the cabin of the aircraft, and then their stomachs rose to their throats as the plane dipped and dropped several hundred feet without warning.

April Adams watched the door separating the passenger compartment from the crew's quarters, expecting it to burst open at any moment. *Had the fight caused some sort of damage to the plane, resulting in the accelerated descent?* But the doors remained bolted.

"Good morning, ladies." A hidden intercom came alive as mist flowed across the wingtips outside the windows. The cabin had fallen silent after the sudden drop in altitude — the four fighting women now lay in a tangled mass in the aisle, some with fists raised menacingly, others with arms around their throats, all waiting to see what would happen next. "We are sorry about the unannounced deceleration, but guerrilla activity along the outskirts of the airport necessitates evasive landing maneuvers. I assure you everything is under control — just a little preventive medicine. Now settle back and buckle up. We'll be on the ground shortly."

Not a single stewardess, April observed as hunger pangs gnawed at her stomach. Once, after Wake Island, a scruffy-looking man with a bulge under his sports jacket walked through to pass out sloppily wrapped, stale sandwiches, but that appeared to be the extent of the airline's services. She realized now she should have become suspicious when initially boarding the craft: it was a huge jetliner, yet it bore no name or logo on the tail, only small identification numbers that were chipped and faded.

The craft shuddered slightly as its landing gear was lowered, and then blackened tenements were rising up outside the windows and the tires screamed and whined as rubber made contact with blacktop. Puffs of wheel smoke fanned out to mingle with the ground-hugging layer of blue smog, and as the pilot channeled fuel into the reverse thrusters, the roaring plane began to slow.

When she felt it turning, April found the courage to open her eyes for the first time since the landing gear had been grabbed by air resistance. Outside the window, long lines of yellow, straw, conical hats bobbed about as workers repaired bombed-out portions of the tarmac. Beneath the sun shields, peasants in black pantaloons and olive-drab, rolled-up shirts labored with picks and shovels while others carried buckets of dirt and debris suspended from poles balanced across their shoulders. Only a few bothered to look up at the passing plane. April noticed their faces were Asian.

"What in heaven's name are *those*?" one woman in the rear of the craft asked the dancer beside her as they watched row upon row of empty concrete hangars pass by. Before the other girl could venture a guess, they observed several more hangars with camouflaged helicopters and fighter-jets sitting inside them and the answer became obvious. Gunjeeps with heavily armed soldiers in flak jackets and helmets that seemed too big for their heads sat every hundred yards or so along the main north-south military runway.

"They look like children," a whisper swirled through the cabin. It was quickly answered with a louder, more realistic, "Don't fool yourself, honey."

A few minutes later, the craft came to a jerky halt, and the women watched three long, black limousines pull up in front of the portable stairwell that was being wheeled up against the side of the plane. "Well, it's about time they showed some fucking class around this joint." The Latino produced her best frown. In the hazy distance, the airport terminal sat beneath the steaming midday sun. Smog-dead palm trees rose up behind it.

"Our own squad of bodyguards," The Texan was pulling her torn outfit back into place and attaching safety pins to strategic seams here and there. Outside, two blue gunjeeps had rolled up beyond the sleek sedans. The men atop them pointed their gun barrels out away from the jet, at the elephant grass swaying in the breeze along the edge of the runway. "They're so . . . *cute!*"

A wave of intense heat rolled in to engulf the craft's already balmy cabin when security men opened the side doors up front.

"My God!" A slender dancer with legs that went on forever loosened the top buttons of her revealing blouse. "It's like hell on earth out there."

"Very aptly put." The cabin door opened suddenly, and a tall Occidental in gray safari suit and reflective sunglasses stepped halfway through the opening. "But I'm sure you will enjoy your stay here with the Association."

"And what is this place?" The no-nonsense Texan fancied herself the unofficial spokesman of the aspiring actresses.

"Your contracts all specified an exotic, exciting

locale deep in the mysterious Orient," he sidestepped her question smoothly. "Most of you, anyway." His smile faded slightly, but the girls could still see the sample of his teeth. "Those who thought they were going to Europe—think again. Those are Asian faces out there. But, if after the orientation scheduled for later this afternoon you have not decided the Paris of the East is a bonus stop in more ways than one, those who choose to leave will be free to do so," he lied.

"You're saying we are not *now* free to leave if we so choose to?" The blond Texan made her way to the door and thrust her ample chest out at him to exemplify her irritation and courage. She was not one to be intimidated so easily by big men with flashy airplanes.

"This way." Mr. Sunglasses motioned the other women to follow the blonde up toward the front of the craft.

"Listen, buster." Her stance told him she was not moving until he gave the kind of answer the passengers wanted to hear. The man's grin brightened and he seemed to rise a couple inches in height as he reached out and grabbed one of her ears.

Dragging her through the doorway, he motioned the shocked girls out of the plane again, and soon April and the others were working their way down the aluminum stairs to the hot, steaming tarmac below.

Something in the air told her a rainstorm had recently passed through the area. Despite the pollution clinging to everything that moved, there was a freshness to the trees and elephant grass waving in the breeze, and the workers a few yards away added to the scent: it was as if she could smell drying garments under the intense heat that had been soaked by a monsoon downpour only minutes before. But there was something else in the air—a sense of danger, of foreboding, that overpowered everything else at the jungle's edge. April felt this was not a town where she could turn her predicament into adventure, laced with intrigue. The place oozed evil. Power she could not see seemed to swirl all about, tingling and tickling her skin while making her lightheaded and filling her with anxiety at the same time. There was an intensity, an electricity, about the place she could not explain—had never experienced before in her life, short as it had been up to this point. Perhaps this was where certain forces of the earth came together and clashed. She did not know.

"Welcome to the asshole of the world." The blonde from Texas lead the procession over to the black limousines. Holding her torn outfit together with one hand, she pulled the scarf from her throat with the other, bothered by the unpleasant heat pressing down on them all. Beads of perspiration rose on the foreheads of the other girls as they followed her. Just waiting for their turn to walk down the stairs from the plane cabin was enough time to wilt most of their skimpy outfits, and devilish smiles broke out on all the security men observing the procession as damp blouses and tank tops began clinging to firm, jutting breasts with revealing results.

April Adams, fanning herself with a folded newspaper she had purchased at the refueling stop in Anchorage, stepped into the middle sedan without protest, well aware she was helpless to do anything against so many heavily armed men at the moment. The limousine had the capacity to seat six passengers in the facing benches behind the driver's sealed compartment, and the blond Texan and saucy Latino were two of those that shared the car with her.

"This really sucks!" The Texan carefully propped up her sagging hairdo, then abruptly gave up altogether. "This sucks to high heaven, I tell ya!"

"I wonder where they're taking us," April asked innocently, regretting she spoke the instant her mouth opened.

The Latino cast her an angry scowl that softened into a big sister frown. "I'd love to give you three wishes, honey. But since I can't, I'll give you three guesses."

"And it ain't Honolulu, *honey,*" the blond Texan served the words soaked in sarcasm and Southern drawl.

April Adams swallowed hard as she watched the driver hand several stacks of colorful currency over to an armed sentry before steering the vehicle away from the airport terminal and waiting customs officials inside.

A few minutes later they exited the airfield through a side gate lined with gun-toting guards and layers of razor-sharp concertina wire.

The driver maneuvered down several winding side streets to avoid what appeared to be police checkpoints, and then the convoy of limousines was passing by the entrance to the sprawling base on its way downtown.

Trying desperately to place the name, April stared up at the huge sign on the terminal wall as they raced past it, dragging the letters into a blur:

TAN SON NHUT INTERNATIONAL AIR-

PORT
  WELCOME TO SAIGON

The four of them sat in the back of the bus. They took up the last row, which was the only bench seat. The two men leaned against the grimy windows. Their women sat between them, leaning on each other's shoulder.

"Have you got to do that in public, Zemm?" Chad Chandler glanced down at his common-law wife and the baby clinging to her exposed breast. "I don't really like the idea of all these total strangers getting a free shot of my old lady's tit." His eyes shifted upward slightly, until they locked on young Cory MacArthur. "You know what I mean, *cherry boy?*" The emphasis he put on the last word told Cory he had better cease staring down at the amber swell of flesh unless he wanted to experience a compound fracture of the arm.

Cory's eyes jerked to the right as he pretended to concentrate on the barefooted peasant girls walking down at the edge of the roadway toward the city, huge platters of fruit and sugar cane balanced precariously on their heads. *Lord, how I love the way their hips sway so delicately, so sensuously to the music in my head.* His smile grew ear to ear and he struggled to hide his face from Big Chad.

"These are my people," Zemm whispered up to her man, not so much with pride as with that ever-present desire to educate him to her ways, though she'd be the first to admit he was a very stubborn man. Even for an American, wherever America was. "These are Cambodians," she taunted him by sliding a hand under the

88

breast and propping it up so that more skin was revealed. "They understand what it it to feed a child on a long journey. They are not embarrassed, nor are they aroused. Would you rather I allow the child to cry, like he did when we spent three hours at that border crossing this morning?"

Chad felt himself growing hard as he watched the tiny beads of perspiration trickle down the valley between her milk-swollen breasts, and he flashed back to those evenings before the boy came along, when they frolicked naked beside the campfires, slick with each other's sweat, making love over and over until the orange glow of dawn found them exhausted and worn raw.

Things were different now. He swallowed the reply rising in his throat and stared at the virgins walking caravan-style down to the Central Market of Saigon. Five or six miles distant. *And they joke there are no cherry girls left in Vietnam,* he laughed to himself. There were definitely a lot to choose from right outside his window. Every last one of them, just about, was pure. He could tell. By the way they walked. And he would swear by it; a woman, no matter how hard she tried, never walked with that flower-petal grace again after she lost her innocence. Not that it really mattered.

Or did it. . . .

The windshield in front of the bus driver shattered without warning—Cory barely caught sight of the long board impacting against the glass before the driver yanked on the steering wheel hard to the right and swerved to the side of the road. Another window up front exploded as a rock flew through it. Several women began screaming. Sporadic gunfire erupted in

89

the roadway in front of the bus, and the driver's hands slowly rose above his head.

Within moments, a squad of black-pajama-clad guerrillas were swarming onto the crowded vehicle.

"Don't move." Chandler held out a hand in front of MacArthur, urging caution, while his other hand curled around the pistol butt riding his hip.

"VC?" Cory's jaw dropped as his arm tightened protectively around the woman on his left.

"Looks that way," Big Chad whispered back.

A Westerner at the front of the bus, clad in a brown safari suit and bush hat, stood up as the soldiers started down the aisle. A rifle butt to the chin sent him flying over two old women who were still seated. His wire-rim glasses slid between feet and glass crinkled as the passengers shuffled about in terror. The man's hair was shoulder length and parted down the middle. He wore his pencil-thin mustache in a Fu Manchu. Chandler thought he looked like a liberal freelance writer from some back-in-The-World left-wing rag out of Berkeley or somewhere.

"I am a reporter!" the two Americans heard him claim. "I just wanted to introduce—" But a boot to the lower jaw sent him reeling again. This time he went silent. One of the old mama-sans bent over to offer comfort when she saw him rubbing his jaw, but with an angry scowl he waved her back.

"We are soldiers of the Provisional Revolutionary Party," the apparent leader of the group announced in Vietnamese. He had not seen the other Occidentals in the back of the bus yet.

"A PR Party-member, eh?" Chandler smiled across at Cory. "That's all I needed to hear. You ready?"

MacArthur responded with a grim, tight-lipped nod.

Several of the soldiers were slinging their rifles at the lack of resistance and producing empty sandbags from packs on their back. "Please consider this an informal get-aquainted session!" The leader bared his gold-capped teeth in a plastic display of friendly brother-hood with his fellow citizens. "We need your moral support."

"And your generous donations," the gang leader's lieutenant added, also smiling as he pointed to the sandbags his men were holding out in front of them.

"Your money, your jewelry," the leader clarified for those dumbfounded passengers with bewildered ex-pressions still on their faces.

"All your valuables!" The lieutenant raised a pistol over his head and fired a shot into the roof of the bus as if to emphasize his point. The discharge bounced back and forth off the walls of the vehicle as a large hole magically appeared in the thin metal overhead, and a cage full of chickens broke free and began flapping up and down the aisle. A woman screamed again, and the child sucking on Zemm's breast coughed and began crying without opening its eyes.

"*A Party?*" Chandler stood up suddenly, brandishing his automatic. The guerrilla leader's eyes went wide at the sight of his towering form emerging from the back of the long bus. "You want donations?" he yelled at the top of his lungs, charging toward the front.

Cory MacArthur was right behind him, a subma-chine gun with folding stock braced against his hip. "Well if this is a party, let's put on some rock 'n' roll!" and he let loose with a short burst of lead that completely ripped the smile off the communist cadre's face and catapulted his frame back through one of the windows in the bus.

Firing quick, evenly spaced, single shots one after another, Chandler took out the four closest men with clean head wounds before any of the guerrillas could even react.

That left one soldier—a young teen-ager near the door who had booted the reporter at the beginning of the siege. Cory took careful aim, intending to fire a single shot at the man's chest, but the Vietnamese was suddenly dropping to the floor, his feet knocked out from under him.

Chandler saw the reporter slamming his telephoto lens against the kid's face as he rushed for the door and fired off the last of his pistol rounds at the guerrillas standing outside. Praying to jungle gods he feared did not exist, Chandler hoped they were dealing with just a small ragtime band of would-be bandits and not a battalion of hard-core grunts fresh from north of the DMZ.

The half dozen Vietnamese squatting at the side of the road scattered, firing back over their shoulders without inflicting any damage.

Cory leaned out the broken side window and sent a sustained burst of slugs after them into the treeline. One man went down with a serious buttocks wound, and through the settling gun smoke, the Americans watched his comrades drag him down into the bloody reeds.

"Do we pursue?" Cory was up beside Chandler in a flash—his chest heaving, his eyes intense, eager for more action. Chandler knew the look: the kid lusted for the kill.

"Fuck no." The ex-mercenary almost laughed as he watched MacArthur slam another clip of ammo into his German-made MP40. "For all we know they got a whole harem of gun-slingin' cunts waiting for us out there, brother."

Cory's worried expression softened as he caught on, and his sudden smile imitated Big Chad's though he was unsure what they were smiling about.

"You were won'ful!" A slender woman was suddenly against Cory, pressing her shapely form to his. He recognized the long, black hair of the Cambodian woman he had been living with the last eight weeks. A strange warmth surged through him, and as passengers all around scurried for the exits, he fought off the emotions that sought to freeze him to the spot so he could contemplate all he had just experienced. It always happened that way after the gunplay. And when a woman was by your side — had witnessed your brief display of heroics — it was worse. His toes felt suddenly damp, and he glanced down at the blood inching across the floor of the bus. It had already crept over the edge of his thongs, and the vibrant color and pulsing of the thick stream sent warning throbs through his temples. *The blood was from a wounded man, not a dead corpse! A heart was still beating somewhere, still pumping.*

Chandler sensed something was wrong as he watched his young partner, and both men pushed their women back away from the aisle and started toward the pile of bodies behind the driver's seat.

A bright flash of light stunned both of them momentarily — they glanced to the right and saw the reporter was pointing his camera at them — and in the field of blue dots that filled their vision, something else appeared. *And it was not aiming anything so harmless!*

Chandler's gun arm whirled to the left and fired without hesitation. The wounded guerrilla, blood still spurting like a fountain from the earlier head wound, flew backwards against his comrades, Russian automatic firing madly into the ceiling as he stumbled, his jaw disintegrated by two, then three hollow-points.

And the whole time the interior of the bus was filling with more exploding flashbulbs and screaming Vietnamese as blood splashed about the shattered glass and crumpled bodies.

"Magnificent! Beautiful!" The photographer kept clicking off shots until the roll of film ran out. He glanced down at his bandolier of film canisters and frowned without looking back up at Chandler or MacArthur. "Damn!" he muttered. "I wish I had had color film in the fucking thing — that was Pulitzer Prize material! Definitely Pulitzer Prize material! But outfuckingstanding anyway! Outfuckingstanding, troopers!" He seemed to be speaking up at the Americans now without really acknowledging their presence.

"Hey." Cory was ignoring the carnage leaking crimson all around him as he went down on one knee beside the photo-journalist. "You think maybe I could get a copy or two of what you shot here today?"

But the reporter was on his feet and rushing about, from body to body as soon as he had a fresh roll in the Rollicord. He never once looked Cory in the eyes when he said, "Sure, sure! That's the least I can do! Hell, the drinks are on me when we get into Saigontown, amigo! The fucking drinks are on me! I'm

94

stayin' at the Continental. Know where that's at?" He busied himself focusing on the grotesque wounds of the dead soldiers. More bright flashes filled the cramped interior of the bus and Big Chad held his hand in front of his eyes.

"Yeah," Cory replied enthusiastically. "Tu Do Street, mate. The Continental's on Tu Do Street."

"Fucking figures," muttered Chandler, disgust in his tone. He did not sound impressed.

"Say!" The reporter glanced up from his work for the first time and looked them over critically. His eyes danced from Chandler's civilian clothes to Cory's. "What unit you dudes with anyway?"

Suddenly it sounded like a monkey had dropped from the trees and was pounding the top of the bus with a ball-peen hammer, but as the chopping vibrations became more distinct, they all recognized the rotor downblast of the helicopter gunship that had floated up across the tops of the rubber trees to hover a short distance above the heavily damaged bus.

An Arvin with a loudspeaker was screaming down from the chopper, and the bus driver, as if to answer his unintelligible questions, was running about outside, pointing at the dead bodies and the numerous blood trails.

"What are they saying, Chad?" Cory was back beside his woman and had her protectively wrapped beneath one arm.

"Something about how they'll stand by until a border patrol jeep gets here to escort us the rest of the way into the city," he responded dryly. Chandler was leaning against the open doorway, watching the treeline through which the guerrillas had vanished, when

95

something made him look back inside, to the rear of the bus.

It was Zemm.

Still clutching their child to her breast, she was watching Chandler from the aisle, looking up at him, that proud sparkle in her eyes as she remained silent, her expression radiating a deep love that had been forged in the heart of the cruel rain forest.

Chad Chandler felt himself blushing as attention in the bus suddenly focused on him and what he had just done. But his expression remained grim and business-like as he pointed at his common-law wife's chest. "Get your tit back inside its blouse, woman!"

7

Manila, Philippines

The red eyes glowing in the dark corner of her jail cell reminded Amy Atencio of pictures she had taken one time using a defective flashbulb—everyone's eyes had come out with a devilish red tint to them. She glanced up at the walls rising all around her; the ceiling was of dreary cinder block, twenty feet overhead, lending a hellish color to the already drab cubicle. The single bulb hanging from a cord in the center was off. Weak shafts of dusk filtered in through the bars of a small window at the top of one wall. Judging from the sounds of traffic on the other side of the bars, she was on the ground floor or second level of the old building.

"Don't go gettin' no perverted ideas, little fella!" She grinned down at the rodent from her position, flat on her back, on a table in the center of the room. And the rat backed up several inches, retreating into the shadows.

Amy tensed her arms, but the straps holding her wrists down to the edges of the steel table were as tight as before she had blacked out. Her legs were still spread too — the ankles tied down the same as the wrists.

One of the little bastards took a few too many liberties while I was out, she decided, straining to look down past the generous swell of her chest to her feet. The blouse was unbuttoned, but still tucked in at the waist. And her trousers were still snapped tight with the zipper up, which was probably the most important thing, though she knew her luck was quickly running out.

She could see the inner edges of her nipples where the blouse was pulled apart. *The bastards ripped my bra right out from under me!* Then she remembered the little weasel with the switchblade and how he had been sliding the knife in and out under the front hasp, in and out, in and out. Before they had slapped the wet washcloth over her face and she coughed, threw up, then blacked out.

It had been an impressive act. All through their threats she had displayed just the right amount of fear and intimidation. And she was confident they were through with her for the night — would be leaving her alone until first light, or perhaps pre-dawn. Then the little bastard with the bucket of water and the washcloth had appeared, smiling just a little bit too broadly.

She feigned ignorance over the accusations, and halfway through the first phase of the interrogation (for Ross had taught them well how the sessions went

98

through four carefully orchestrated parts), a high-ranking police official burst in, condemning the torture and relieving one lieutenant of his command — at least that's how it all sounded from her rather precarious position beneath the water-clogged towels and the suffocating washcloth. Countless boots had shuffled in and out of the room, and the restraints were briefly removed. "This is not how things are done here in Manila!" she overheard one commander reprimanding another in the hallway outside, but then her savior was marching away, and she was flat on her back again, groaning almost imperceptibly as the restraints were reapplied. *And with a vengeance!*

They had let the tarantula walk around on her face for over an hour — it never once saw fit to bite — and twice they threatened to fill her vagina with vicious army ants that had been whipped up into a frenzy. But when all was said and done the only thing she was really subjected to was the water torture.

"Just tell us who sent you here!" they demanded over and over. "Just tell us which unit abandoned you downtown. We *know* you are with the American military! *Talk!*"

She wondered if Ross and Collins and Sewell were ever picked up after they dragged her away from the hotel, but she knew they hadn't been for she had heard one of the officials out in the hallway being reprimanded for allowing her "associates" to slip away without also being detained for questioning.

"Just tell us what your mission in the Philippines was!" they demanded to know, and she had promptly allowed her nausea to overcome her. She lost consciousness long before any answers were forthcoming.

"Tomorrow!" She could barely hear the interrogator yelling down into her swirling, black pit. "In the morning you shall talk! In the morning your flesh shall taste the bite of the wires, *bitch*!"

The wires.

Faint pangs of memory tugged at her mind as her temples throbbed with pain.

The wires.

She could remember the woman back in Saigon. The American woman. The actress they had strapped down just like she was now tied to the table. The traitor they had hooked the field phone up to.

A field phone was a portable communications system that connected base stations with outposts or distant bunkers — and that distance was no obstacle, so long as you possessed an abundance of electrical wire to connect everything together. Each field phone contained its own hand-generating device that powered the unit without the need for batteries or a foreign energy supply. The terminals could be tampered with so that the electrical charge fed to the ends of two hot wires. And those tips could be connected to anything: fingers, toes. Tongues or testicles. A woman's breasts. Or the lips of her crotch.

Amy would never forget the look on that woman's face when they poured the juice into her. It had been disgusting. But it had been war.

And the woman had been the enemy. A traitor — the most despicable of the species: a double agent. Amy

100

could remember what the communists had done to the girls of her village, so many years ago, south of the border, in Guatemala. And when she thought about those times, and after she endured the nightmares that always followed the daylight memories, she felt less and less compassion for any female who worked under-cover for the Red Menace.

Now the tables had turned. Now the cold steel table propped *her* up as she lay flat on her back, so vulnerable to her interrogator, her legs spread wide for him, her limbs strapped down, rendering her fists and heels useless, regardless of her anger or motivation or . . .

There it was again!

Outside the window. The noise. Like branches breaking, or rocks sliding down a steep hillside.

Sounds one would hear if a captive princess's knight in shining armor was trying to climb the castle walls without rousing the slumbering dragon.

Amy's eyes closed, exhausted. She was in the middle of Manila somewhere. The noise was that of a pack of rats as it rummaged about the piles of debris outside, searching for food. Horns blared as traffic jammed only a block away. She was not in the middle of some enchanted forest, miles from the scattered civilizations of old England. She was flat on her back in a dirty torture chamber—one of a dozen identical cubicles in this same wing of the Filipino dungeon, no doubt—in a sprawling, polluted, high-decibel city of over six million, and she was an inconsequential slab of flesh in the complex swirl of things, so why worry about it all, anyway?

101

She slowly dropped her head back against the harsh table top in resignation. Perhaps this was release. Perhaps this was finally the end of it all. Death.

And life after death.

Visions of cathedral spires and robed priests and old women praying in the front pew flooded her head, and she wanted to cross herself, but the bonds held her arm down. She remembered the Catholic teachings that had been with her all through childhood, and she remembered the faith that had seen her through the long journey north.

And she remembered all she had done alongside the war dogs. All she had seen. All that had happened to her over the lifetime that was only a few miserable months, really. Yet during this last year she discovered something she had only suspected while working the cold streets of New York City: there was no God.

And if he — or she — existed, a woman of her lowly rank in the order of things surely deserved no attention from the Supreme Being.

As all these thoughts swirled through her head like a mangled collage of conscience, guilt and remorse, Amy gave up hope. This was where it all led to — where it would all end. On a table top in a dark dungeon on the other side of the world from where her ancestors had all been murdered.

And she really didn't give a damn. *She really didn't care anymore!*

"Let it be finished!" she screamed at the top of her lungs, feeling so alone now, and helpless, that the dark no longer frightened her.

How nice it would be to have your friends at your side, a voice in her head mocked her with a sardonic little laugh, but she ignored it even as the faces of Brent and Justin and the others flashed before her. She had always been alone in this life—even when the nights saw an unknown john passed out in her arms. Even when Brent was snuggled up beside her. Can't let them get too close. *Can't let anyone get too close!* Love lost can only cause more pain, more sorrow.

She would leave this world as she had entered it: alone and abandoned.

But the screeching of metal against stone tugged at her consciousness again, summoning her from the deep pit of darkness. Something outside.

Someone was at her window! She opened one eye, almost fearfully, and saw the fingers clutching the thick bars. And she recognized Brent's ring as a street light's sparkle was reflected off the carved silver.

"Amy!"

The harsh whisper flooded her veins with energy she thought had drained from her forever.

"Amy! It's me! *Collins.*"

"Brent!" she called back weakly. "Are you crazy?" The question seemed silly for some reason, and she wondered why she even bothered to ask.

"Are you handcuffed?" another voice called to her, barely above the din of passing traffic outside. She recognized Matt Sewell's voice instantly.

"They've got me strapped down on a table," she replied, laughing aloud now. "They've got me tied to a steel plate, Roscoe! Just like we fried that old Wanda bitch back in Saigon! Just like . . ." Warning lights flashed in her head, and she fell silent, suddenly cautious, but no sounds came from beyond the bolted door. The guards down the corridor had not heard her.

"Are you injured?" It was the lieutenant's voice. Amy thought perhaps she had never heard anything that sounded so good before. The tone exuded power, confidence. *Salvation.*

"My savior has not forsaken me," she whispered under her breath, her eyes locked on two opposing cracks in the ceiling that ran together to form a cross above her chest. "My savior has not forsaken me," she repeated the words reverently, amazed at her own tone, frightened by the implications of it all. Was she referring to Christ? Ross? Or God's actions on earth through, in this case, the three soldiers outside who had come to rescue her? The thoughts bombarding her head overwhelmed her, and she settled back in the pit again, losing grasp of reality.

"Amy! Are you injured?" It was Ross again.

She did not answer immediately, but the question floated in front of her mind's eye in bright red neon.

Was she? Not really. They had slapped her around a bit and, true, the water torture had sent her to the brink, mentally. But had she sustained any disabling wounds? Not yet.

But it seemed all she had gone through this last week, all she had suffered: the theft of her property, her passport — *her identity!* (false as the cover name was) — the inability to go to the U.S. embassy for help (that alone constituted abandonment, it seemed), tor-

ture at the hands of a goon platoon of renegade thugs
. . . it all seemed more cruelty than she could bear.
Than she could endure, alone, without the war dogs,
as much as she abhorred them, to back and support
her. Yes, she was injured. *Psychologically!* And she
feared it was a wound no doctors would ever be able to
save her from. Amy began envisioning herself locked
up in a mental asylum, and tears flooded her eyes
uncontrollably.

"Amy! Can you hear us?" It was Matt, master of the
Huey gunship—her guardian angel, descended from
the cloudy skies to save her! "Are you injured, hon?"

"I—I'm OK," she said. "But I can't move, guys."
Suddenly everything was back to normal. The tears
had stopped. The bonds holding her limbs down were
a mere nuisance—something the men outside would
free her from. The weight that had been pressing down
on her from the heavens was gone. She was back to her
old feisty self.

What had all the crying been about?

She was mad. Angry a bunch of macho-mentality
Filipinos had managed to strap her down to this table
without a hair-pulling, groin-booting fight. And she
just might punch that Roscoe out for letting them take
her out of the hotel in the first place!

"They've got both my arms and legs strapped down!"
she continued, pausing to hiss down at the rat that had
grown closer to monitor the whispered conversation.
The rodent scurried back into the shadows, its red-
light eyes disappearing as it retreated.

"How far are you from the wall?" Ross's voice

reached through the bars at her again.

Visions of an old cowboy movie where bandits tied ropes to jailhouse bars, then pulled them out with the aid of a horse flashed through her head briefly. "About ten feet or so!" she called back uneasily. "Why?" She could hear no horse neighing outside or grating its hoofs against the ground impatiently. "What are you guys up to?"

"We're gonna huff and puff *and blow this wall down,* baby!" Collins laughed despite the dangerous situation unfolding.

"Can you find any cover at all?" Sewell asked hopefully.

"There's *plenty* of cover in here!" she said sarcastically, "but like I told youz guys—I can't move! They've got my ass strapped down to a table top, for Christsake!"

"What if the shrapnel tears off her chest?" She overheard Collins anticipating the worst as he spoke with the others outside her cell.

"Any more than a mouthful is just a waste anyway," Ross whispered back, loud enough for her to hear, and Amy gritted her teeth in anger, fuming now.

"I'm gonna kill youz bastards!" she threatened loudly, and footsteps started down the corridor in the direction of her cell.

"Turn your face away!" Ross directed. She could already hear Collins and Sewell running away. "We've set the charge low. It should send any stray shrapnel beneath table level. *Good luck, baby!*"

And he was gone that quick.

"Roscoe!" she called out at the top of her lungs, sure she was about to perish any moment in a searing blast. *They sounded drunk!* "You sonofabitch! Come back here!"

Why? she asked herself, regaining control of her mental facilities once more. Why were they doing this ridiculous stunt?

She was in no danger here! The fiends torturing her were not part of the recognized government authorities, but misfits who had happened to capture her during one of her weaker moments and who would slink back into the shadows when that corrections officer returned in the morning to ensure they had released her as he had ordered. Somehow these people were connected with the communist sympathizer she had been trying to frame — whose five daughters had in turn successfully manipulated fate and contrived a scheme against her.

It would all be straightened out in the morning! *Why was Ross screwing everything up like this?*

The blast caved in the bottom of the brick wall and sent a cloud of billowing dust and debris rolling under the table beneath her. When it met the opposite wall it climbed up toward the ceiling and mushroomed out over her, settling across her face and making her cough violently.

The door to her cell burst open and, without bothering to look inside to assess the situation first, an automatic rifle was poked into the cell by a young guard and a sustained burst of tracer fire was unleashed in a bright horizontal fan, inches above Amy's quivering, conelike breasts.

Most of the rounds ricocheted out through the gaping hole that had appeared in the far wall.

A metal canister flew into the cell, rolled along the floor, and as it bounced off the wall, CS gas started spewing forth, filling the room with an irritating silver cloud.

Sewell leaned in and sent a short burst of soft-nosed slugs at the doorway. Lead arced down off the bricks onto the cement floor with dull thuds.

"Christ, Roscoe!" Amy screamed. "Youz clowns are going to get me killed!"

Collins rushed into the cubicle and, commando knife in hand, began slicing through Amy's bonds.

"I want their heads!" A tall Filipino appeared in the doorway, yelling. He had a .45 automatic pistol in each hand. "I want every one of their heads!" And the doorway became shoulder-to-shoulder uniforms.

A submachine gun barked twice, and Ross—just entering the hole created along the bottom of the wall—was lifted off his feet and thrown backwards. A slug had caught him in the right shoulder.

A heavy rifle barrel came down and cracked across Collins's back and he dropped to the floor, dazed.

"Brent!" Amy screamed. "Brent!" But her voice was drowned out by the din of boots rushing into the cell from the corridor outside. Her head turned to the right and pressed flat against the table. She saw the bottoms of two boots disappear through the gaping hole that had been blasted into the wall—Sewell was dragging an unconscious Ross back out into the night.

"Your friends made a big mistake, trying to free you from this facility!" An open palm slammed against the side of her head. Amy's eyes exploded with stars that were immediately engulfed by an all-consuming mist. "I guarantee you that all of you will regret the day you stepped foot in the Philippines."

Boots rushing past toward the hole in the wall sounded like pounding sledge hammers, and her temples began throbbing. Amy turned her head to the other side and glanced down at Collins.

The ex-policeman was not moving. His face was caked with blood. He reminded her of the dead sailor she had just left a few hours ago, lying in a back alley off Roxas Boulevard. The thought filled her eyes with sudden tears, moments before the rifle butt slammed into her jaw, knocking her out.

8

Saigon

"I don't do *that* kind of dancing." April Adams was adamant as she stood in the dressing room at the rear of the nightclub. She glanced down at the tissue-thin string bikini in her hands, then back up at the man in the doorway.

"You don't have much of a choice in the matter." He folded his arms across his chest and smiled.

"What do you mean by that?" April dropped her hands to her sides, and the light garment sliding across her bare thighs caused her to shudder. Things were in no way developing the way she had hoped and anticipated.

"Unless you can flap your arms all the way back to The World." The man's grin brightened. "And that isn't very likely, now, is it, miss?" He was dark complected and looked South American, but April wasn't sure. He stood nearly seven feet tall and had a weightlifter's physique, but perhaps it was just the smaller stature of the passing Vietnamese in comparison that made him look so monstrous. He wore tight-fitting khaki pants tucked into brown leather boots, and a loose fencer's shirt with the sleeves folded up above the wrists. His head, shaved bald and glistening from the heavy evening humidity, came to a shining point at the top. He reminded April of a bullet.

"Well, I'm not going out there wearing only this," she repeated. "You can see right through it!"

"That's the idea." Bulletman scratched his thin mustache as if suddenly hungry for her. He liked what he saw standing before him. April was clad in a pink miniskirt that came up to the tops of her thighs. Her reddish-blond hair bounced lightly atop bare shoulders, unaffected by the suffocating heat. Her youthful chest was restrained by a halter top that appeared several sizes too small — the fabric constantly rubbing her skin about with every movement accented the fullness of her breasts by keeping the nipples taut and bothered. Bulletman couldn't help but drool over them — it was obvious they had never been put to the use they were created for. His eyes dropped to her long, sleek legs. High heels pushed the firm muscles into sensuous shapes. The outfit she wore was what they had supplied her that morning when her luggage "turned up missing." She didn't like it much more than the bikini.

"You shouldn't be so temperamental," Bulletman laughed at her frown. "Without a passport, you don't have many options, now, do you? This is the Nam, honey. You need all the friends you can get."

"Speaking of that." April sat down on the edge of a bench and crossed her legs impatiently. Her thighs tensed provocatively, and Bulletman felt himself growing hard. He did not attempt to hide the bulge. April avoided staring at the obvious development. "I never did get to talk to the police about the theft of my papers. Are they ever going to show up—when did you call them? Or should I ask, *did* you call them?"

"I wouldn't worry about the authorities right about now, young lady." Bulletman's smile faded and his brows grew grim. "You should concentrate more on earning your plane ticket over here!"

"Vietnam wasn't really on my itinerary." She matched his scowl defiantly. "I was supposed to be a dancer in Korea, *chump*! For the USO! I was supposed to get help improving my singing, so I could advance professionally, so I could grow. And I'll tell you one thing: this ain't Korea. And those old farts slobbering over the young Vietnamese girls out there sure aren't GIs at a USO show!" In the background, drumbeats sent the walls vibrating, and customers in an adjacent room could be heard cheering on a floorshow stripper.

"That's *two* things." Bulletman started toward her suddenly and April jumped back off the bench, startled.

"What are you *doing*?" she whimpered in pain as he grabbed her arm and she tried unsuccessfully to twist free. "Let *go* of me, you ape!"

Bulletman grabbed the front of her halter top and tore it open, and April screamed as her breasts popped forth, suddenly free, but nobody came, and they bounced about wildly as the two of them struggled around the room awkwardly, stumbling over furniture and crates of black-market goods. As they rushed past an ancient desk in one corner of the room, Bulletman grabbed something off the top, and then he was wrapping both arms around her waist from behind and forcing her down onto the floor.

"Leave me alone!" April pleaded, aware she was helpless under his immense weight. "Please let go of me!" But he ignored her, forcing her face against the cool teakwood planks. April's chest flattened out across the floor. *"Please!"*

Bulletman slid his knee between her thighs and forced her legs apart. He hiked her miniskirt up around her waist and ripped off her undergarments as if they were made of plastic. Then he pulled a long syringe from the case he had removed from the desk top, and plunged it into the femoral artery near her groin. April screamed again and never ceased resisting, but only a few more seconds passed before she seemed suddenly sapped of her strength, and her limbs went limp.

"What . . . did . . . you . . . do . . . to . . . me?" Her voice was an exhausted, dreamy sigh, and he could feel every muscle in her body relax as he slid his pants down to his ankles and rammed himself deep into her.

Her insides resisted briefly then split apart, and though she didn't cry out from the pain of penetration, Bulletman knew he had just forced his way into a

113

garden previously guarded from all suitors.

"What . . . did . . . you . . . do?" she repeated, more weakly now, a smile spreading across her face as he dropped his full weight onto her and she shifted her hips about underneath him to accommodate his thrusting pelvis. It was obvious she did not really know what was happening to her.

"You now know the pleasure of the Big H." Bulletman closed his eyes as he cupped both her breasts from behind and plunged into her harder and harder. Flesh slapped against flesh as he ran his lips along the nape of her neck, basking in the knowledge he had conquered virgin territory, wallowing in the transfer of youthful power such lovemaking was rumored to bequest the taker.

"The Big H?" April's smile vanished when she felt herself fill up with him as his loins exploded. She felt suddenly sick all over, terribly soiled, dirty, despite the rush coursing through her veins and the silver wings trying to lift her mind up to the clouds.

"*Horse.*" Bulletman let out a deep gasp as he purged the last of his sickness into her, and then he collapsed onto her back, his face buried in her piles of fluffy hair fanning out across the floor. "Just pretend you're riding the big white horse up to heaven." His body shuddered one last time as he shifted about on her small frame, comforting himself from the harsh teakwood, uncaring and oblivious to her own suffering, if indeed the heroin was allowing her to suffer at all.

"Horse," April repeated the word slowly, as if aware of the implications closing in on her, yet powerless to

114

do anything about it. Those silver wings were pulling her away again, and she felt free, despite the heavy weight pressing down on her.

"Just unwind and enjoy it, baby," Bulletman whispered softly, licking her ear. "By the time we're through with you, by the time we've showed you all the ropes in this business, you'll be one of the most sought-after 'entertainers' in the Orient," and he allowed a little laugh to escape him.

"Here we are," April spoke slowly, grasping at the words swirling around in her head, "in such a compromising position, Mister . . . Bulletman. And I don't even know your name." She felt totally detached from her surroundings now—on a different plane entirely. She could not even feel the weight of the heavy man atop her, though she could clearly see his stocky frame—almost as if from above. It was like she was floating in a distant corner of the ceiling, impartially observing the goings-on inside the room.

"My friends call me Cotton," the Bulletman revealed during a moment of weakness. She was shifting about beneath him with dreamlike movements now and the sensation was driving him crazy.

"Cotton?" She drew the two syllables out as if she were unable to remember what mental pictures the word was supposed to conjure up. Though her limbs refused to respond, she saw herself sitting on a small, white cloud with a golden lining. With her hands she was patting its shape together and fluffing it up while her bare feet poked through the bottom of the filmy gauze and almost touched the naked couple writhing about on the brown, barren floor. "You said . . . Cotton?" Her lips were no longer moving but her thoughts took on sound without coaxing. "What kind of name is Cotton? You're not even *black*!" And she heard herself laughing hysterically.

"But my friends *call me* Cotton," he replied, hearing her affront somehow. His tone told her they were both not participating in the same conversation.

"And am I your friend, Cotton?" She tried to turn over so she could draw his hardness deeper within her.

"No," Cotton said matter-of-factly. "You're not, bitch," and he twisted one of her breasts until she cried out. His free hand slid down and slapped her legs apart even farther, and he pushed in with all his strength, jabbing her viciously, trying to hurt her, but all she did was turn her head to the other side, submitting to him, powerless to resist, drained of strength. "You're nothing now, cunt," he continued to insult her. "You're trash. You're scum. You're less than the dirt under my feet when I walk out to a battlefield latrine."

"So . . . cruel." April Adams sighed again as she vaguely felt her body being pounded down against the hard teakwood floor. "You don't have to be so cruel."

"Cruel?" Cotton the Bulletman laughed loudly and his massive arms crushed her delicate shoulders together as he reached his second climax. "This is nothing, baby. Wait till you meet the first string of customers we got lined up for you."

* * *

"So here we were," the well-known reporter lifted his drink for emphasis, "landing in a formerly hot LZ, the scent of napalm still fresh on the sticky breeze, charred and blackened crispy critters lying all around, knee-deep, sporadic incoming mortar rounds still kicking up dust on our flank . . . and this crazy Cavalry captain saunters up to our gunship without so much as a flak jacket on, sporting an ear-to-ear death's-head grin. He offers what appears to me to be an enthusiastic handshake, so I take hold of it — *and his whole arm falls off!*"

"What?" Zemm had been listening attentively to the war story, trying to grasp all the unfamiliar words being used. Chandler and young Cory sat on either side of her, noncommittal expressions on their booze-flushed faces.

"Yeah, no kidding!" His hands flew up in a *would-I-jive-you?* gesture. "But it wasn't really *his* arm at all. It belonged to one of the fuckin' VC — pardon my French — tunnel rats his unit had just gunned down in the firefight that had raged from pre-dawn to just prior to our arrival. I mean to tell you: I laughed my ass off!"

"Pardon your French again." Big Chad cast him a dirty, annoyed look and slid his arm around Zemm's shoulder.

"Right, of course. Sorry, mate."

Cory MacArthur glanced past the reporter's shoulder after nodding with a tight smile. He felt obligated

117

because of the promised free round of drinks—but he did not laugh outright. He had heard variations of the same tale numerous times in bars throughout Indochina. He was no longer impressed.

The three Vietnamese women on the stage were swaying back and forth in unison with each other, Hawaiian style, to the beat of a slow Hugo Montenegro tune. Clad in see-through bikinis that hugged the cracks of their haunches, they all stared down at him, obvious invitations to Oriental heaven sparkling in their exotic, almond eyes, competing for his glance—running their long, sharp fingernails up along sensuous curves to spawn a thirst in him only they could quench. But he refused to lock eyes with any of them—Cory concentrated on their bodies below the throatline, comparing chests, and marvelled at the difference in vibes. Measuring bouncing bustlines was no different than casually judging porno paintings along the back alleys of Tu Do, but locking eyes with these Asian women brought on an intensity that would start the adrenaline and other juices flowing. It was a process that never ceased to amaze Cory. He felt he did not possess the energy necessary to choose one and follow her home to her dark and sparse tenement hooch. Instead, he went from one set of breasts to the other, imagining his face pressed up between them, smothered by the soft, warm flesh. *Only a soldier has the privilege to choose the place, time and manner of his death.*

"Yes, it was one hell of a landing zone." The reporter reached across the table and tapped Zemm on the arm lightly. Chandler shot a mental bullet at him but did not physically react. "These GIs are a laugh a minute. I don't care what the goofy Brits say, I'd take this Nam quagmire over the cold war in Europe anyday."

"I think I'm in love." Cory was rising to his feet and unbuttoning his shirt.

Zemm's eyes went wide at the sight of his exposed chest, even though she knew he was referring to one of the dancers up on the stage, and not her.

"Here we go again," Chandler sighed in resignation as he reached up, clamped a hand on the kid's shoulder and pulled him back down into his seat. "Happens every time we breeze into Saigon. Something about these *Veeyet* women, I guess, though—for the life of me—I can't understand what."

"Cambod' women make much better wives," Zemm agreed, smiling playfully at Cory now as she elbowed her common-law husband appreciatively. She turned back to Chad and her soft doe eyes misted over with unabashed affection.

"I wasn't huntin' for a wife." MacArthur stood back up as soon as Chad released him. "Just a whore!"

Swaying from the effects of the alcohol on his short, thin frame, he bounded away from the table before he could be restrained a second time.

"I'm gonna have to clip his wings or deck his young ass before the evening's over," muttered Chandler in an irritated tone, but he remained in his chair for the moment, carefully nursing his drink.

Cory was up in front of the dancer in the middle within a couple seconds. Her long, black hair shimmering like rare silk beneath the flashing purple-and-

119

red stage lights, the woman's tissue-draped breasts seemed unusually large and jutted out at him as if propped up and squeezed together by invisible supports. They were smooth and firm, curving upright at just the right angle, like an artist's erotic sculpture. "Ahhh—" the student of Greek mythology licked his lips and made a deduction—"the miracle of silicone injections! Where have you been all my life, *manoi*?"

The woman stopped gyrating to the sudden beat of a new, faster song, and stepped to the edge of the stage, her feet apart now in a challenging stance. She braced her hands on shapely hips and grinned down at him mischievously. Cory watched the tips of her breasts quiver to a nervous stillness in imitation of the rest of her unmoving curves, then he reached up, wrapped his hands around her buttocks and buried his face in her crotch. "I love you!" he yelled in Vietnamese, and though bouncers started toward the stage from different ends of the bar, nightclub patrons at the front tables cheered him on loudly.

The dancer took hold of her bikini's lower seam riding one leg and hiked it up several inches so Cory's mouth could find the moist meat it hungered and hunted for. The crowd went wild, and when the girl arced her head back in mock ecstasy and moaned in tune with the accelerating music, the joint nearly erupted into a riot.

"Here we go again," Chandler's frown took on storm shadows as he slowly rose to his feet.

The doors to the establishment swung open just then, and Big Chad's heart skipped a beat in apprehension when he saw the white letters glowing faintly on the black helmets.

MPs.

Some of the bar customers displayed a noticeable drop in their exuberance also but, for the most part, the din of cheers inside the huge, concrete cavern failed to wane. A few heads turned curiously as the squad of six military policemen made their way through the crowded tables to the front stage. Four of the six were smiling grimly at Cory's *savoir faire*, and they just stood behind him for several seconds before making a move that might set off the boisterous crowd.

Finally the tallest MP, buck sergeant stripes on his green jungle fatigues, nudged Cory in the small of his back with a black rosewood nightstick. "I think it's about time you retreated to your table, trooper." The NCO produced a fatherly mask. "Before that tigress eats you up whole." Two of the MPs laughed good-naturedly, but the other three looked like they wanted to leave with MacArthur's scalp on their web belt.

Cory's hands shifted to the woman's smooth flesh along the inside of her hips and he pushed her away roughly. As she stumbled backwards, startled, and tripped, plummeting onto her tight bottom with a sharp cry, the kid whirled around with his fists raised.

The closest MP, a short, stocky Puerto Rican, produced a pistol in the blink of an eye and had it up against the kid's nose even before his jaw could drop. "I suggest you mellow out, pronto!" The private's voice was sharp as a knife blade plunged through warm butter, and it carried through the backdrop of rowdy

121

bar patrons just as distinctly. "Drop the knuckles or lose those baby-face blues!"

Cory had no way of knowing the MP did not have probable cause to use deadly force and was only bluffing, hyped up by the intensity of the crowd closing in on them. This was Saigon. Bustling capital of a nation at war. War meant sudden death. It was a place where anything goes. And it was all he knew.

His fists dropped, and an embarrassed smile slowly crept across his features. "Aw, shit, guys!" He brushed the .45 aside and draped an arm over the MP's shoulder. "I didn't mean nothin' by it. I'm just delirious from lack of cunt juice, know what I mean? I thought you were a bunch of locals, intrudin' upon my space. Let me buy the PM's boys a round of drinks!"

The buck sergeant slid his nightstick into its keeper and insisted on straight pineapple juice or ice coffee for his men—booze was out of the question. "That's one thing I always tell my troopers," he toasted Zemm with a wink of his eye. "Beware of the three B's, for they're the root of all evil among cops: booze, broads and bets. Gotta watch your ass when dealing with any of the above." He tipped his helmet to Zemm. "Present company excepted, ma'am."

Zenn smiled, blushed and turned away, afraid to check her husband's expression.

"Yeah, *women!*" Cory agreed before tilting his head back and swallowing an entire bottle of Vietnamese *33*. "You can't live with 'em, and you can't live without 'em."

"Where have I heard that one before?" One of the

MP enlisted men turned to his fellow private, frowning, and they both glanced back at their sergeant.

The reporter who had been sitting at Chandler's table earlier left his seat and ventured across the bar in search of fresh company upon seeing the law-enforcement personnel make their grand entrance. He and the sergeant exchanged hostile looks as they passed in one of the aisles. Neither Cory nor Chad missed him — the fool had bought total strangers three rounds of drinks, and that was all that mattered.

"Was that my favorite foreign correspondent I just saw sitting at your table?" the sergeant asked Chandler sarcastically as he sipped a baggy of ice coffee through a long, colorful straw. "Darnette?"

"I think that's what he said his name was." Chad wrapped his arm around Zemm protectively as the MP took the seat across from them the reporter had abandoned. "The dude didn't really impress me that much. You know how them clowns are: all talk and no action. But I guess you can't really fault them — that's what their job is all about."

"Bloodsuckers." The sergeant gritted his teeth.

"What?"

"If that's what their job is all about, then they should get into a respectable line of work." He sucked up the last of the strong, black coffee and kept draining on the straw for several seconds afterwards. "Fucking poges."

Chandler smiled at the contradictions, puzzled but not prepared to waste time pondering the MP's words. "I'm afraid I don't catch your drift, friend," he said anyway.

"Darnette holds a U.S. passport," the brooding soldier explained, "but he's about as American as Russian vodka." He blew air back into the baggy through the straw and slammed his hands against it, sending a loud pop through the structure that instantly silenced several nearby tables. "The sonofabitch is about as left-wing liberal as the scale goes," he went on with an expression that said, *Wasn't me who made the noise!* "But then again, they're all commie sympathizers, if ya ask me." Chatter at all the nearby tables quickly resumed when no explosions, smoke or falling ceiling rafters followed the loud bang.

Chandler's brows furrowed in concentration. "Now that you mention it, the name is starting to ring a bell, Sarge."

"He's the same douchebag that's been writing all the bummer articles critical of U.S. involvement in Indochina."

"That's the dude!" Big Chad slammed his fist down on the table top angrily as he recalled a story he had read in the paper on the long bus ride down from Cambodia, but he did not mention the incident with the VC guerrillas. War stories were a dime a dozen. He didn't think the MP with the bullet hole scar in his ear was in the mood to listen to any.

"He'll volunteer to go out on gunships with the grunts, my friend—only to come back with a story that portrays the GIs in the worst possible light. And it's always the same, it doesn't vary with the circumstances or mission. Hell, one time he accompanied a Lurp team up across the DMZ. One of the Green

124

Berets got a CMOH out of the op, yet *he* had the gall to write up a BS story that made our heroes look like crazed rapists and baby killers."

"They should've hung him by his balls in Charlie's territory and let the guerrillas have him." Chandler's eyes burrowed into the back of Darnette's head as the reporter, fifty feet away now at another table, flirted with two bar girls.

"That's just it!" The MP held up his hands in resignation. "The bastard doesn't *have* any balls!"

"It's not really your fault." One of the younger MPs joined them and picked up a beer-drenched newspaper lying across the table in front of it. "You couldn't have known."

"We just met the dude on the bus coming down." Chandler nodded his head in relieved agreement, biting his tongue before adding anything about the Cambodian border. "He wanted to buy us a round of drinks—I think he just had the hots for my wife here." He tightened his armhold around Zemm, making another point with her and sending a subtle, unmistakable hint to the MPs the girl was taken.

Zemm was watching Cory with a disapproving smirk. The kid had left his Cambodian girlfriend back at the hotel (she had complained of the jitters and a throbbing headache after the incident on the express bus, and didn't want to go out on the town so soon after their lengthy journey), and she felt he should have remained behind with her. Yet here he was trying to devour a dancing hooker who knew more tricks than he had whiskers. "You American *men*!" she grumbled under her breath, so soft the others at the table could barely hear her.

"What's that, honey?" Chandler leaned over and pressed his lips against the hair covering her ear.

"Hey! Check this out." The MP was sliding the edge of his hand across the soggy newspaper like a squeegee, forcing the beer out as he flattened it for better reading.

"What now?" the MP sergeant muttered bitterly. "I suppose they're announcing an end to the war." The statement came across sounding more disappointed than hopeful. Chandler gave the grim-looking NCO a critical once-over. He appeared to one who did not really know him to be the kind of man who had found a home in The Nam and never wanted destiny or circumstances beyond his control to bring to an end his street-gray paradise.

"Naw, Sarge." The younger cop didn't look up from the story that had caught his interest. "Better than that: some Korean War vet back in The World made the front page. Suffering from postponed shell shock, or something like that."

"Sounds like another one going bananas on us." The sergeant reached over and scooped up the reporter's half full glass of bourbon and downed it in one gulp without bothering to glance around to make sure no one was watching. The period to his statement was an *I-don't-give-a-fuck* belch.

"Not quite," the private continued, ignoring his supervisor's antics. "Seems the guy was fighting severe bouts of depression, and had even attempted suicide

126

twice — something about guilt over having survived the war while so many of his buddies perished on the battlefield."

"Survivor's guilt," Chandler mumbled, his smile fading. Zemm glanced up at him, a deep sadness in her eyes. It sounded like her man was speaking from personal experience.

"They've got all that in a fucking international newspaper?" The sergeant leaned across the table slightly, trying to focus on the upside-down print. The black-and-white file photo of the veteran involved was covered with beer, and he felt the uncontrollable need to protect it from further defacement. "All that loony-tunes talk put down in print? And with his name in the same story?" His tone showed growing anger.

"I'd sue," Chandler decided. "I'd sue the motherfuckers for every penny their commie editor-in-chief's got stashed away in Moscow!"

"Naw, guys — it's not all that derogatory. The story actually makes the dude look more like a hero than anything else. Let me get to the point — this is quite a write-up."

"So get to the point." One of the other MPs was still standing behind his sergeant. Now and then he glanced about apprehensively, keeping careful tabs on the bar patrons. His black-and-white MP helmet made favorite targets for drunk GIs. More than once in the past, beer bottles had been tossed at it by an unseen, anonymous "hero." The bar check had run its course and was intruding on borrowed time. He hated mingling with intoxicated loudmouths who always felt obligated to confront a military policeman to show their girls how brave they could be.

"Anyway." The MP with the newspaper reached over and swiped an untouched baggy of pineapple juice and began sucking on the straw protruding from it. "Apparently the guy was undergoing therapy at a rap session held by a shrink whose brother had been killed in Korea by the Red Chinese, right? So subliminally or something, the doc plants the major plan in our vet's head, OK, gentlemen?"

"The major plan?"

"Hey, this is great!" The MP with the newspaper was reading a paragraph ahead of each development before he related the story to the others at the table. "So our vet hero thinks all this therapy crap is a crock of shit, right? But the shrink doesn't fail completely, OK? He instills in our main man a sense of purpose in life — a goal. Why kill yourself for nothing but the sake of suicide, you know what I mean? If you can't put up with life's little hassles — not that this survivor's guilt you mentioned is a little hassle, sir." He glanced over at Big Chad apologetically. "But if ya gotta pull the pin, so to speak, why not go out with a big bang, right?"

"A big bang?" The MP sergeant's brows came together in deep concentration. Chandler thought he looked burned out on policework, or maybe the Saigon smog had finally fried his brains and now he was just going through the motions until he had his big-20 in the bag.

"Our hero wrapped himself up with dynamite, C-4 and a whole rucksack full of frags and walked into the

Communist Party headquarters in New York City and shot the place up with two automatic rifles."

"A man after my own heart!" Chandler raised his beer bottle in honor of the hero.

"Wonder if I got enough leave time saved up to fly back for his funeral," the MP sergeant said seriously.

"That's just it!" The private with the newspaper was tearing the article away from the rest of the text so he could save it. "The dude took out a couple dozen ABCs before some of New York's finest rolled up on scene and wrestled his young ass to the ground!"

"ABCs?" Chandler looked puzzled.

"American-born commies." The MP sergeant sounded bored as he continued staring down into his empty glass without looking up.

"Anyway, a bunch of rich, right-wing lawyer-types have volunteered their services to the dude. And you know how our wonderful American judicial system operates," he said sarcastically yet with unhidden optimism.

"The judge'll let him off on an insanity defense." A smile cracked the hardened MP sergeant's face.

"Right! Heck of a way to get a body count back in The World, but I'm afraid Uncle Ho might not share our sense of humor over this escapade."

"The vet oughta get a medal," Chandler said.

"I just hope they don't give him the chair," the MP with the newspaper article folded it, stuffed it down in a thigh pocket and stood up to leave.

Moments later, a small, metallic object flew in through the front door and bounced off his helmet, knocking him back off his feet. "Frag!" he yelled on the way down as the smooth sphere of steel rolled under several tables before coming to rest between the feet of a Chinese businessman from Cholon.

"Grenade!" Chandler threw himself on top of Zemm as everyone at the table dove from their chairs and upended the table for cover.

The explosion that followed was deafening in the enclosed confines of the nightclub. Shredded limbs from the Chinaman's table rained down on the Americans and the orange lanterns suspended from the ceiling above each table flickered on and off for several seconds before going out altogether, throwing the huge building into total darkness.

Several yards from where Chandler lay atop Zemm, women were crying softly as smoke fanned out across the cavernous room, but there were no screams. And no secondary explosions. The single grenade was the beginning and the end of it. For tonight.

Such was terrorism in Saigon, Pearl of the Orient.

"Are you alright?" The MP sergeant was going from Chad to Cory, then to his own men. "Are you OK?" He sounded much more concerned than he would have been at a routine bombing. This murderous act was something he was taking personally. Innocent people had just died painfully because some punk with poor timing had attempted to take out a squad of military policemen in a public place.

"Yeah." Young Cory MacArthur pushed himself up off the floor and began dusting himself off. *Where have I gone through all this before?* he wondered silently. "I think we're all okay."

But the MP sergeant was gone after quickly deducing the same. Automatic pistol drawn, he was rushing to the door in pursuit of the unknown assailants. He was gunning for trouble, chasing after the VC alone like that, but Chad felt no obligation to assist him. Zemm was safe, lying uninjured beneath him, and that was all that mattered anymore in his life. He could see the sergeant pausing in the doorway now, eyes darting back and forth down both sides of the dark, deserted street. The Cong were long gone. Which way should he go?

Zemm lay unmoving beneath her husband, listening to the sirens pulling up outside. Her teeth chattered in mild terror, yet she felt safe under Big Chad's crushing weight. She wished they were back in their hut at the edge of the rain forest clearing in Cambodia's deep wilds, but she knew it was her duty to follow her man wherever his travels took him. It was just that she had heard so much about Saigon — how the women were so beautiful, what with their fancy clothes from Paris and their facial coats of makeup . . . how fountains with multi-colored spotlights at their bottoms lit up the misty nights in front of the fancy cinemas downtown . . . how there were horse races at a place called Phuto, whatever a horse was (the only races she had ever seen involved cockroaches the size of mice) . . . how there was a presidential palace much like Princess Raina's, back at the Khmer-guarded cliff wall, but that this one was in the heart of a city of three million people. *Three million!* (Never in her life had she had to

131

count that high for any reason) . . . how there were huge markets in the midst of all the crowds and sputtering motorscooters where you could choose from vast aquariums of scurrying crabs and lobsters, and watch the chefs cook them right before your eyes. But nobody told her people might try to kill you while you sat drinking in a secluded bar. Or dining in an open-air restaurant.

The other MPs lying around the table were rising to their feet also now, and rushing over to back their leader outside. One was losing blood from a throat wound like a water faucet with a bad leak, but he appeared to be ignoring the injury as he drew his sidearm, eager for action. Chad nodded his head in pity; he knew the kid felt no pain because adrenaline was coursing through his veins at full-speed-ahead. After things calmed down a bit, his world of hurt was going to sneak up behind him like a sledge hammer. But, for now, he was feeling no pain.

"I love you, Big Chad." Zemm shifted around beneath her husband as his arms lifted him up slightly to better watch the professionals in the doorway. She reached up, wrapping her arms around his neck, and hugged him tightly. "You save me tonight—again. And I love you forever, honey."

Chandler looked down at his woman for the first time since shielding her from danger without really thinking about it. She was shivering with fear now, and her eyes were dark pools of terror and anticipation, but Zemm wore a forced smile across her lips. "I love you too, baby." He lowered himself back onto her

132

gently and they kissed passionately as people all around sobbed or groaned in pain. Blood was advancing across the smooth teakwood floors in vast pools, but neither of them seemed to notice when her long, silky hair became soaked along the edges with it.

9

Manila, Philippines

Brent Collins woke with his head throbbing and his eyes swollen shut. Out of instinct, he automatically brought his arms up, to pry them open, but chains rattled, and the wrists moved only an inch or two before the slack grew taut, restraining them firmly. He was sitting on a cool cement floor, his back propped against a brick wall. His legs were wedged tightly in a heavy wood block that had two holes drilled through the middle.

Using his shoulder, Brent rubbed his right eye open, ignoring the stinging pain and the blood and pus that oozed down onto his cheek.

He was in a dimly lit cell, weak shafts of sunlight through window bars near the ceiling providing the only illumination. From their angle, filtering down through the floating particles of dust, he judged it to be about three or four in the afternoon.

Startled, a silent gasp escaped him when he saw Amy in chains, hanging against the far wall from wrist manacles connected to iron stakes protruding from the cinder-blocks. Her hair coated with dust and her face streaked with tear-lined soot, she was unconscious, with her face hanging down against her chest. She was not naked, but her clothes were in such shreds she might as well have been. But Collins could detect no injuries from where he sat on the floor; they had not beaten her because of the aborted rescue raid. Then he swallowed as a queasy feeling swirled through his gut: these islanders had a way of torturing you that left no telltale marks on the outside. Only psychological scars.

"Amy!" he whispered, after listening intently for any movement outside the cellblock door. "Amy, can you hear me? *Amy!*"

The Guatemalan beauty stirred slightly, then slowly lifted her head to meet his worried gaze. There was fire in her eyes, even so soon after regaining consciousness.

He thought perhaps she had never really blacked out, but had just been resting from the ordeal of the last twenty-four hours.

Twenty-four hours. Had it only been that long, or had they been down in this dungeon for weeks?

"You stupid bastards really got us into the shitter this time, Brent baby," she muttered, lava and poison mixed into her tone. Brent wondered if the hate was anything personal. They had once been so much together. He hoped she was just in a bad mood over the unexpected turn of events.

"You're on your period, right?" He smiled up at her naively, and Amy kicked her feet at him viciously in reply — held off the ground several feet by the manacles. The act was not only futile and useless, but almost comical as far as Collins was concerned.

135

"Fuck you, asshole!" she lashed out at him like a striking snake.

"Aw, Amy." His head bobbed about like an embarrassed Cub Scout at the profanity and verbal attack. "Remember your training. We gotta cooperate with each other, work together, if we're gonna get our asses out of this one, right?"

Atencio's position softened when Collins didn't respond to her cursing with something along the lines of how he'd love to let her have sexual intercourse with him if it wasn't for all the restraints separating them. Her angry scowl faded, and she focused on the blood dripping from where one of the guards slammed a rifle butt into his face several times. "Are you alright?" She sounded genuinely concerned for his well-being.

"Now that's how I like to hear you talk." Collins tried to broaden his smile despite the pain lancing through him. "Soft and gentle, the way a woman should. I *knew* you cared, after all."

Amy's frown returned, but she did not insult him again. "I'm sure we'll be out of here soon," she said hopefully. "When that corrections officer finds out what they've done to us, heads will roll. This is not really the way they do things in Manila—not to the good guys, anyway!"

"You're living in a fantasy world, baby!" He laughed up at her. "This is Asia! The Far East! Some foreigners don't come *back* from here, my dear. Let's be realistic. Even if there's some shining knight out there in a correction officer's uniform that would risk repercussions from his men by coming to our rescue, do you think he'd know where to look? Glance around you, Miss Atencio! This isn't the same cell you were in when we tried to rescue you the first time. We've probably been transferred to another cell block on the other side of the complex. Hell, we might be on an entirely different *island* altogether! The man would never find us."

"At least we're still above ground," Amy said optimistically.

"Do you mean above ground as in not down in some dungeon, or above ground as in not yet in our graves?" But he didn't give her time to answer. "Face it, cutie —" he was speaking now like a purely professional partner and not a man she had made love to a hundred times in another life, another place — "we're marked for death. It's only a matter of time."

Amy bit her lip. She didn't even know what had been about to come out, and she didn't want to say something corny or stupid. Her eyes fell to the ground, tears began cascading down her cheeks and her breasts took to shaking slightly with each wave of sobs that racked her body.

Collins, frowning deeply now, shook his head from side to side in resignation, ignoring the stabbing pain that poked at his temples. "Aw, Amy, *come on*! Knock it off. You know I hate to see you cry — it's just not convincing. In fact, it's downright comical. You've killed too many dirtbags to break down and cry over something as minor as this."

Brent's battlefield psychology — or grim sense of humor, some might call it — worked. The gut-deep sobs stopped, as did the tears. Several seconds passed, then Amy looked up, met his hopeful gaze and began laughing. "Guess I can't fool you, can I?" she said.

Collins conceded victory to her. "Almost." His smile

returned. "But no cigar. Now let's get down to business. What's our first step going to be in getting out of this hellhole?"

Amy seemed to consider the question, as if for the first time. Her face registered puzzlement. Collins knew the look. She was genuinely burnt out on the stress. Her mind was not functioning as smooth and sharp as it usually did. She wanted someone else to figure things out, someone else to find their escape route, someone else to lead them past the jail cell bars. "You're asking a slain dragon lady for advice?" Her attempt at jailhouse humor failed miserably.

But Collins appreciated the gesture nonetheless. "A dragon lady you're not," he said, trying hard to ignore the creeping sensation as more and more blood trickled down along his cheek. "I'd say you're more like a captive princess any man would give his life for. Dragons be damned. I don't care if this *is* their domain—I'm dedicated to the belief we'll survive this one, Amy." He willed her eyes to meet his again. "Just like we beat the odds on all the rest. The Philippines should be a piece of cake compared to what we've been up against in Vietnam and Cambodia. We've got more than camp spirit and unit pride going for us, baby." He couldn't believe the way their conversation was sounding more and more like a pep-rally duet. "We've got love."

"I missed you, Brent," she finally admitted. "My little R&R here to Manila hasn't been a party by *any* stretch of the imagination."

"What about all the gigolos you were flying out here to bed down?" He feigned intense hurt, but she knew he was only mocking her.

138

Approaching steps silenced both of them, but the guard in the corridor outside was only making his hourly rounds, and his footsteps soon faded in the opposite direction from which they came.

Amy waited a few more minutes, testing the silence, before she responded to his allegation. "I spent every night alone," she admitted in a tone that told him only someone very special even deserved to know. "Oh sure, I dined in the hotel restaurant, and had my share of Don Juans and Casanovas glide by trying to kiss my knuckles, but no one worth a damn bit at the bait."

"In other words, no one more dashing than yours truly." He bowed as best he could, in view of the primitive restraints.

"Correct," she conceded a third time to him, almost laughing aloud that they could be discussing such an immaterial topic as love and feelings when they were in a torture chamber, awaiting surprises only hell's own sentries were privy to. "I really missed you, Brent. But I never, in my wildest dreams, thought it would end like this."

"I had rather hoped to get my ticket cancelled on the battlefield during a raging firefight, I must admit — not die from old age chained to the stocks like this."

"I'm sorry, Brent." Her tone revealed troubled guilt.

"It's not your fault." He was twisting and turning his wrists in a futile attempt to get free.

"It's *all* my fault! If you guys hadn't answered my cable for help, none of this would have happened."

"You'd still be in the shitter." Collins ignored the pain as the decades-old wood rubbed his wrists raw and started them bleeding. "Eventually that bastard with the five conniving daughters would have come and got you. It's better this way—at least some of us are still together. We're a *team*. We'll die together!"

Amy was in no mood to participate in such defeatism. "Ross will be back to get us," she said, the confidence in her voice plastic, phony.

"Ross is dead," Collins stated coldly. "I saw him take a chest wound with my own eyes. Them dudes in the doorway were firing heavy-duty shit, baby." He was working furiously on the manacles now, not bothering to look at her anymore.

"Blood," Amy said. "Did you see any blood?" Collins did not answer her, but kept struggling with the stocks. "No, you didn't. And neither did I, because there was no blood! You guys were all wearing body armor under your coveralls, right? Just like normal?"

Collins pulled one arm free suddenly, and he glanced up at her, a bright and satisfied grin across his dirty face. "Yeah." He drew the single word out as if he had just swallowed a mouthful of beer after several days in the hot, steaming jungle. "Body armor." Amy wasn't sure if he was more happy about jerking an arm loose or the prospect Ross had not perished after all.

"And Matt was there with him," she continued. "Was there to help drag him away even if he *was* more than just stunned by the blunt trauma of the round!"

"Whatever you say, doll," Collins growled as he wildly pulled on his other arm with the free limb. For some reason Amy thought of a timber wolf with its paw caught in a bear trap, viciously gnawing through the leg bone with its teeth, trying anything to get free from the steel jaws. "But listen to the noises coming through that tiny window up there, will ya?" He finally succeeded in jerking the other arm free, and he set to work pulling the planks on both sides of his legs apart. "I'd judge from the sound of them—the honking horns and the screeching tires and the grinding bus engines—that we're still in Manila. But they're distant, baby—can't ya tell? We must be at least ten or maybe even twenty floors above the ground. Now how's Roscoe and company gonna mount a rescue mission against those odds?"

Wood finally splintered, and he broke completely loose of the ancient contraption. "Fuckin' finally!" he muttered, wondering for the first time if perhaps the cellblock was bugged with electronic listening devices. *Naw, they weren't that important a catch*, he decided.

"I can still hear that train passing by every couple hours down there, to the east," she said. "So we must still be in the same building, wouldn't you think?"

"There's trains all over these islands, Amy." He started over toward her, only to stumble flat on his face—his legs and feet were still numb from so many days in restraints. "Well *fuck me!*" He sounded on the verge of tears himself now. He sounded, to Amy, like he was in terrible pain, but she had not heard bone crack.

Amy gasped loudly when Brent tripped. She wanted to ask him if he was alright. Instead, she said, "But it's the same train."

"The whistle?" he slowly rose to his hands and knees, patiently waiting for the blood to circulate in his lower limbs before making another attempt at crossing the room.

"No," she replied. "The way the engine sounds as it approaches. It's got a broken wheel shaft or it's warped or something. *Click click click, clack clack clack, it's gonna*

141

break!" She practically sung the words to him in a cadence that made him laugh out loud.

A train was passing by below even then, as they spoke. "Yeah." Collins tilted his head to one side, listening intently. "And there's that peculiar music the tracks play every time a train rolls over them—you know what I mean? I guess every stretch of rail is different. It sounds the same, gives off the same metallic twang each time a train passes by."

"Like now."

They both listened to the train race past below their jail cell somewhere. It was a long mining train. The music lasted several minutes, and they listened to it as if it were a favorite record from a treasured collection of oldies.

"Well at least we know we're in the same building." Collins slowly rose to his feet, testing his balance before starting toward Amy again. "For whatever value that knowledge is worth." He did not sound optimistic at all.

"I have faith in Justin and the others," Amy smiled warmly as her ex-lover drew closer. "They'll make it up here, by hook or by crook."

The closer Brent came, the more visible his torn eyelids got, and she felt the nausea taking form in her stomach, but she refused to look away. "Oh, Brent . . ." She wanted to reach out to him, to mother him, to love him like she had never loved him before.

"Don't bank on it," he replied to her statement about a rescue attempt. "The old man back at the Big P just wouldn't authorize all the bucks necessary for Roscoe to bring the rest of the boys over here for a—" and he snickered—"show of force. It just wouldn't be cost effec-

142

tive. No offense, honey. To me, your tits are worth their weight in gold, but that's only my opinion, ya know what I mean?" He laughed lightly as he reached her and gently ran the back of his hand along the side of her face. Even after all this time in the dark confines of the cell, she smelled good to him. His hand slowly dropped, turning as it did, and brushed across her breasts, lingering at the lower edge of her nipples. Patches of amber flesh showed through gaping tears in her blouse. His other hand lightly touched the mound where her legs came together, and the nipples quickly grew, pushing forth through the slits in the thin fabric.

"Now I know why they call this a torture chamber." He bent forward slightly and licked at one of the nipples, cupping her crotch with his hand at the same time and massaging it expertly. "A guy like me could really take advantage of a girl like you — in a situation like this." He place his mouth against the breast over her racing heart and took as much between his lips as he could.

"Just get me down from here!" she demanded, smiling helplessly as he sucked loudly at her flesh, exaggerating its pleasant taste. "And quit making so much noise, you fool!" she reprimanded him playfully, suddenly forgetting all the pain they had been feeling only moments ago, "or the guards will hear you!"

"Milk!" he gurgled against the tips of her breasts, the warm flesh pressed flat against his face, hiding his eyes. "My kingdom for a cup of milk!"

"These boobs got nothing but *Cuervo Gold* in 'em, buster!" She flexed her chest at him.

"I was hoping for Muscatel, baby," he replied loudly, ignoring the threat too much noise brought on. Amy tried to kick out at him, but her ankles were held back by the chains protruding from the iron stakes in the wall, and his testicles were spared.

The restraints were not held to the stakes with a padlock, but merely looped around them in such a manner the prisoner was unable to free him or herself. After a few more minutes of teasing the bound Amy with his oral skills, Brent reached up and lifted the loops free. He draped her over his shoulder, then, using the backs of her thighs for support, pulled away from the wall with slow, but powerful jerks. The iron stakes, corroded from decades in the tropical heat, eventually slid free from the crumbling cinder block.

Exhausted from the exertion, Collins stumbled backwards awkwardly and fell onto a pile of stained and beat-up mattresses that were being stored in the cell.

"You'd think they would have been kind enough to spare just one of these for the two of us." He opted for conversation as she rolled off of him and they came to rest side by side, facing each other. "Considering all the nights we been lodged in this honeymoon suite together."

Her face, inches from his now, gazed into his eyes sadly. "I'd be content learning just how *many* nights we've wasted in this dive." She went along with the game, but then she couldn't hold back any longer. With her hands, she gently cupped his face. "Your eyes." Tears started flowing from her own again. "What in God's name did they do to your eyes?" and she burst into sobs again.

Brent embraced her tightly. "At least I can still see through them." He searched for something good to talk about. "I mean, at least they didn't make me cross my heart and hope to die so they could stick needles in my eye." His grim humor was beginning to be too much.

"Just hold me," she said, burying her face in his chest.

He gently pushed her over onto her back and began sliding her prison pants off.

She sighed in resignation. "Not *here*, Brent! Anybody could walk in at any time." But she did not resist. "We're in *jail*, for Christsake!" She searched for another reason that he might listen to and she tried desperately to ignore the sudden realization she was growing moist where his free hand had gone to work on her. "You're injured, honey. We shouldn't be doing this. It might make things worse. You might have *internal injuries!*"

"*You're* gonna have internal injuries if you don't shut up and spread those thighs!" he joked, whispering harshly into her ear as his hands struggled with the last of her clothing. "This might be our last chance to do it before they lop off our heads!"

"Real romantic, Brent." She frowned as she took hold of his growing hardness hanging down from the torso suspended above her and guided it in. "Real fuckin' romantic."

"Exactly, baby." His arms bent at the elbows and he lowered himself onto and deeper into her. "Now you're catchin' my drift," and he ran his lips back and forth across her chest as he plunged in and out with his hips, basking in the sudden heat of her, and growing increasingly light-headed as the jail cell filled with her soft whimpers and groans of rapture.

* * *

Guards were rushing to the rooftop, drawn by the roar of the flapping rotors.

"We haven't got much time!" Ross bit his lower lip nervously as his trigger finger massaged the submachine gun in his lap. The Hog-60s hanging in the Huey's open side hatches were unmanned.

"Are you sure that whore down in the bar gave you the right scoop?" Sewell held the chopper in a noisy hover directly across from the tenth floor of the prison.

"She wasn't a whore!" Ross snapped. "She's a secretary for the constabulary — or so she claimed. It took twenty bucks' worth of booze just to get her to admit that much!"

"I just hope you got the right info, Roscoe!" Sewell armed the fire controls.

"Just blast the fuckin' building, Matt!" Ross watched his chopper pilot expertly maneuver the craft to just the right angle parallel with the tenth-floor barred windows.

"Woulda been nice if you coulda got a better location — like *which* cell they were transferred to!" Sewell looked both irritated and challenged, the latter brought a hungry grin to his face. The Fly responded to his every move, like a jungle animal born in captivity but constantly restless. They were like one when the rotors flapped.

"It was hard enough just getting the floor number," Ross muttered, rubbing his jaw for emphasis. "It took over four hours in the sack and the utilization of my most professional talents and skills."

Sewell was somewhat relieved his lieutenant was relaxing finally. *But right before the shoot?* "Your tongue must be killin' ya!" he laughed.

"Yeah."

"Here goes." Sewell gritted his teeth and aimed the often-unpredictable nose cannon. "I just wonder how many of the wrong prisoners we're gonna knock outta their racks before we find the ideal couple."

"Just start on the end there, and work your way right to left." Ross's eyes were glued to the increasing number of guards rushing to the roof to see what all the commotion was about. "You sure you got the right rounds in that damn thing?"

"Trust me." Sewell grinned like a demon just released from Pandora's box.

The helicopter bucked ever so slightly with the muffled *thump* and they watched the blur of a round fly across the fifty yards between the wall and the chopper in a slight arc.

The grenade impacted against the cubicle on the far end of the tenth floor, and after the smoke cleared and the shrapnel dropped to the ground far below, a jagged hole appeared in the bricks the size of a Volkswagen.

Ross, his right shoulder still smarting from the bullet wound that was only a nasty bruise thanks to his body armor, activated the ship's powerful spotlight, and as the beam shone through the gaping cavity, they could see male Filipino prisoners diving for cover inside.

"Wrong one, Einstein!" Ross muttered as he shifted the beam of hot silver up at the guards on the rooftop. They'd start shooting now any moment.

"No shit, Sherlock!" Sewell swiftly blew out the next cellblock wall, and after the silver-and-black smoke had cleared, numerous dark-complected faces appeared in the charred opening, staring out stupidly at the flapping monstrosity hovering in the night.

"Strike two!" Ross yelled, firing a short burst of red tracers up at the roofline to drive the guards back for cover.

Sewell did not answer this time, but concentrated on shifting his sights on target number three. He did not waste mental energy wondering if The Fly's nose cannon was inflicting shrapnel wounds. This was the only way—their last chance and final-ditch effort at rescuing Brent and Amy. Another week, and the pair would either be dead or rotting away in bamboo cages on some prison island out in no man's land. The rounds he was using were high-concussion, low-fragmentation choices that would shatter a weak wall—like the ones that made up this building—but retain little power to do additional damage afterwards. Sewell loved them. They were great for strafing palm-frond huts frequented by the VC in the Vietnamese countryside.

The ship lurched again slightly, and a third grenade shot out at the wall while Ross sent another five-round burst of glowing lead up at the rooftop, one floor above them. For some reason, the guards had still not returned the fire. Ross himself was not shooting to kill—his tracers were all directed at the base of the rooftop veranda, which also housed a small heliport. Using pistols with silencers attached, they had punctured the lone craft's fuel tanks before attempting this mission, though they felt it was highly unlikely the Filipinos would give chase using the small, black Loach on the roof—Ross's informal intelligence source also advised him the camp's only helicoptor pilot was off on extended sick leave after a crash over communist-controlled hamlets in the southern islands two weeks earlier.

The round impacted squarely in the center of the third cubicle, throwing a sheet of orange flame back out at the chopper as a section of bricks caved in, revealing the prisoners inside.

"That's them!" Sewell yelled, ecstatic — only a dozen seconds had passed since they fired the first grenade out the ship's nose cannon.

"Yeah!" Ross laughed at the top of his lungs as he sent another burst of tracers up at the rooftop. "I'd recognize that ass anywhere!"

And he directed the spotlight across the pale buttocks of Brent Collins, still thrusting madly between Amy's spread thighs, her feet high in the air.

10

Her lips drawn back away from her teeth, Amy gasped as Brent pulled out of her—roughly and without warning. Her body tingling madly, she brought her legs together, bent her knees and curled up into the fetal position before rolling over onto her side.

"Come on!" Brent latched onto an arm and began pulling her to her feet. "It's Matt and Roscoe!" He shielded his eyes from the powerful beam of light playing across their naked bodies and dragged her toward the gaping hole in the wall, smoke drifting in front of it. Beyond the shadowy form of the helicopter hovering in the air outside, a backdrop of sparkling stars shone brilliantly. Dripping wet, Amy made no attempt to cover herself.

"My God!" Sewell, back in the pilot's cabin of the chopper, blinked his eyes rapidly upon spotting the well-endowed female inside the cell. "I never realized she was so stacked, Ross!" The helicopter started to drift to the left slightly as his concentration was broken. *"That's Amy?* Our Amy? My God, I'm in love!"

Ross frowned at Sewell's antics and, feeling himself grow suddenly hard at the sight of her breasts bouncing firmly with each footfall, shifted the spotlight away — back up at the rooftop.

"Aw, Roscoe!" Matt sounded upset though his words were laced with resigned humor. "Throw some light back on that masterpiece of nature! *Gimme some tit!*"

Ross ignored him, electing to throw some tracers up at the rooftop instead. The Army lieutenant was grinning proudly, more than satisfied with the final product. Amy had not flown to Manila looking for a Latin lover. Not in the beginning anyway. She had just told Brent that to make him jealous. No, Ross had finally sent her here for that plastic surgery he had been promising her since she was first recruited into the war dogs.

Amy had come to Ross's attention in New York in early 1963, after she singlehandedly killed a madman the police had been unsuccessfully hunting for months. Known to the news media as the Bronx Basher because of his weakness (or passion) for slamming his assault victims (usually street hookers who he had sliced up with an ice pick) into the sharp edges of granite or marble buildings, the monster had been impersonating a police detective in order to get the ladies of the evening into his car.

Amy had been tricking in the Big Apple due to circumstances beyond her control. A refugee from war-torn Central America, she had no skills, except those that came with the world's oldest profession.

She had quickly come to learn the rules of the street, and the laws of survival in the big city. And she had not been easily fooled by the Basher's ploy — the maniac had to grab onto her flowing hair and drag her into his automobile.

The curbside kidnapping was witnessed by two *authentic* undercover officers working surveillance on a nearby rooftop, though by the time they came to Amy's assistance, the young, pretty Guatemalan needed no help. She had blasted the Basher to hell and back with her Saturday night special, but not before he had nearly slashed one of her breasts off with the razor-sharp blade.

The scar ran from her throat to her belly. Her tricking days were over.

And the authorities wanted to put her away on a murder rap. "The first two or three shots were justified, miss," the detective had said, smiling down at her in her hospital bed while the doctor pulled the flap of meat that was her breast back in place and stitched it up with ugly crisscross sutures. "But reloading the cylinder as you calmly watch blood pour from the faggot's eye sockets and then going to town six more times is premeditated murder."

But Ross had appeared out of nowhere—while the painkiller still had her in a state of mind too confused to make coherent decisions, she always insisted when joking with her brother war dogs—with his promise of freedom and his little goddamn contracts.

Just sign on the dotted line. She could still remember Ross's conniving death's-head grin. *As you'll note, the ink's in blue and not blood red.* But it had turned out to be a life sentence anyway.

Ross sent another burst of hot lead across the edge of the rooftop and waited until the look on Brent's face told him what he wanted to know. "OK!" he motioned directly overhead. "Take it up!"

Brent Collins wrapped his prison shirt around Amy

as they huddled next to the hole in the bricks. "He's pulling away!" she screamed, holding the shirt tightly closed across her throat and breasts—the cool downblast from the helicopter's rotors was incredible. "He's leaving us!" She bent forward and looked down. Traffic had snarled in the narrow street ten floors below. Horns were blaring. Distant faces looked back up in her direction—at the hovering chopper, its constant drone now taking on increased power.

"No!" Brent caressed her shoulders from behind, trying to comfort her as they stepped onto the broken bricks along the bottom of the gaping crater. "He just doesn't want to hit the side of the building with his rotors, Amy! He's pulling up above the rooftop so he can hover directly over the side of the building!"

"What fucking good does that do us?" she screamed back at him, competing with the deafening *whop-whop-whop* of the blades that measured fifty feet, tip to tip.

"My bet is they'll lower a rope ladder down to us then!"

"This dump has got guards!" she argued. "Did you forget that? They'll shoot their ass out of the sky!" She clutched his upper arms and tried to shake him back and forth, furious with the escape plot. "Why couldn't they just come up the goddamn stairs?"

"I love the way your boobs bounce when you get angry." He locked eyes with her.

Amy slapped him. Harder than she had ever slapped any man before in her life. "We're going to die here, Brent! We're going to die here and you stand there making wisecracks about my fuckin' tits!"

Brent's smile instantly faded. "It's because I don't know what else to do, baby," he said so softly she

153

almost didn't hear him. The slap had sent a spray of blood from his swollen eye. Hating herself for hitting him, she relented and wrapped her arms around him. She wanted to cry again, but this time the tears would not come.

The instincts for survival were wakening her to the situation now, and everything around them — the smoke, the sounds in the street below, the scent of their lovemaking, the downblast of the rotors — was taking on an almost-haunting crystal clarity.

The scent of their lovemaking. When he had entered her, the feeling had been as dreamlike as the nightmare they found themselves trying to escape. But they partook in it almost feverishly, completely losing themselves in the passion of it — using the sudden storm of emotions and feelings to hide from the reality of their surroundings, to run from the dangers lurking beyond the door. Hand in hand, they had dashed so deep into that mental safehouse that when the explosions sounded outside and the walls began to shake, they never even took notice until the bricks of their own cubicle crashed in around them.

"There!" Collins pointed out at the night. The rope ladder was suddenly dangling in front of them.

He reached out and grabbed hold of it, then looked up above before leaving the safety of the shattered wall. Ross was showering the rooftop with scattered bursts from his submachine gun. Collins realized the lieutenant wasn't out to kill any of the guards — but the Filipinos didn't know that.

"Let's go!" He leaped out onto the ladder and swung away, leaving her behind.

"Brent!" she called, throwing empty hands out to

him.

When his weight brought him swinging back against the building, she jumped, and he caught her in one hand. "Hold on!"

Feeling the chopper tilt to one side slightly under their combined weight, Matt Sewell glanced down. His people were aboard.

Banking sharply to the left, he swooped down between two tall, leaning tenements, alive with cheering tenants crowding its flimsy balconies, and vanished in the dark of night, Brent and Amy still swinging fifty feet below the belly of the craft on the end of the rope ladder.

Her head hanging out the open hatch of the chopper as it banked in and out of the lancelike apartment houses rising up all around, Amy could tell by the draft rushing through the craft her haunches were visible below the hiked-up edge of the shirt Collins had wrapped around her. But she didn't care. She didn't care how much of an eyeful Lieutenant Roscoe or that pervert pilot Sewell got. She was hyperventilating — for the first time since she could remember — and the only thing that helped was holding her head out the hatch and sucking in the hot, sticky breeze swirling across the islands like a thick, wet gauze.

"You'll be alright, baby." She could feel Brent pulling the tail of the shirt down along her thighs. She knew she should be feeling a sudden warmth toward him for his loyalty, but she just didn't care anymore.

They were free of the prison.

All that mattered now was starting over. Somewhere

else. Anywhere but Asia.

"You two put on quite a show down there!" Matt Sewell laughed as he buzzed a military installation on the eastern edge of the island, then finally ascended up into the low blanket of rain clouds. Amy wasn't sure just what he was referring to. And she didn't care, so she just remained silent.

"Up your ass with an entrenching tool, Matthew!" Collins cast him a tight smile. He touched his fingers to his lips, then brought them down to within an inch of Amy's buttocks before aborting the love tap — she never saw what he was doing behind her back — and both men exchanged knowing winks.

"Do you think you could direct me to the villa of that dude who caused you all this grief, Amy?" Sewell called back over his shoulder.

She brought her head back into the craft for the first time, barely catching his words because of the roar of turbines overhead. "What do you mean?" Hope gleamed in the depths of her eyes then abruptly faded. *If he was toying with her, she would kill him right on the spot — the crash be damned!*

"Oh, the ol' Dragonfly's got a couple air-to-ground missiles left in her pods. I was just thinking maybe we could jettison them into the asshole's backyard or something."

"That's out," Ross interrupted as he slammed a fresh clip of ammo into his submachine gun. "We've got these two out of their predicament, now it's back to the Nam. Vengeance is sweet, but it'll have to wait for another time. I wanna get back before Big Chad and Cory-*san* kill a king or something."

"Aw, have a heart, Roscoe!" Collins cast the stone-faced Army lieutenant a mischievous grin, but Ross's bullet-gray eyes made his throat go dry. He had to work at keeping the expression intact. "That's what life is all about! We gotta—"

The chopper suddenly began a sharp ascent, and the abrupt change in angle sent everyone against the floor with their stomachs against their tonsils. "Excuse the interruption!" Sewell was not trying to be polite. "But we got company!"

All heads turned to the rear of the helicopter, until a hazy line of non-stop yellow flashes came into view a hundred yards behind them.

"The Loach!" Ross yelled at his pilot. "The fucking Loach from the prison rooftop! What went wrong, Matt?"

"So the dude returned from sick leave without extending the courtesy of telling us he was back. Typical personnel fuck-up, Justin!" Sewell's ability to sound sarcastic and subdued regardless of the current crisis never failed to amaze Ross.

"But we shot up the chopper's tanks!" the lieutenant countered.

"Even them Loaches carry a lotta fuel, boss!" he yelled back above the whine of straining rotors. "It probably hasn't all leaked out yet!"

"But they shoulda noticed the smell when they piled into it! That whole rooftop musta been flooded by now!"

"Hey whatta I look like, a fortune teller?" Sewell took his eyes off his flying for a second to glance back at Ross. "How do I know what happened back there? Maybe the damn thing's got self-sealing fuel tanks for just such events. Bullet holes, that is."

Ross thought that over for a second as Sewell fought to pull away from the hornetlike Loach. "I unloaded enough tracers onto that rooftop to burn down half of Manila," he claimed, but as the craft banked sharply to the left he concentrated on holding onto the metal supports protruding from the wall.

The M-60 machine guns, hanging from the door hatches on empty ammo bandoliers that had fiberglass wires running through them, swung about wildly with each evasive maneuver Sewell brought the Huey through. "Grab a Hog!" Ross directed Collins to one of the powerful weapons. "Fifty bucks says you can't blow that piece of shit out of the sky before me!"

"You're on!" Collins leapfrogged over Amy so fast he almost flew head-first out the hatch. He grabbed onto the M-60 and sent a wild spray of lead out in a fanning motion from the side of the chopper. Every fifth round was a glowing white tracer. None of them came anywhere close to hitting the Loach.

Ross laughed uproariously, despite the threat of imminent death chasing their tail rotor. "What a pussy!" He lifted the breech mechanism to make sure the belt of 7.62 slugs was seated firmly then slammed it back into place. "Let me show you how a *man* goes target shooting!" He swung the weapon back around as far as it would go, but could not bring a bead down on the pursuing Loach due to the angle.

"Forget it!" Sewell called back over his shoulder again. "You'll never hit the bastard — not if I can't get him in front of my mini-guns!"

"Then turn the tables on this chase and freak the sucker out!" Collins called back. "Fly a loop-de-loop or something! Impress me, Matt. Give it all you got for a change!"

"It's not that easy!" Sewell descended rapidly, then banked sharply to the right, barely avoiding a sustained burst from the Loach's weapons systems. "But I got a better idea! Tell me about the sonofabitch that got us into all this, Amy!" he screamed back at her. "Tell me about his pad! You made the dude sound like a real fancy playboy! Tell me something I can use!"

"What?" She stared back at him dumbly. Her face had lost all its color. She looked like she was about to throw up. She had lost contact with the rest of them — with reality, if any of this could be called reality. She wasn't comprehending anything they had been saying.

"The villa, baby!" Collins rushed over to her side and grabbed her, catching what Sewell was up to. "What side of the island was his mansion on?" Ross made no verbal objections but his eyes narrowed noticeably.

She hesitated only a second before seeing the urgency in Brent's eyes. "It was just a few blocks from the Manila Hotel." The words came from her automatically, without even thinking.

The chopper swerved to the left, barely missing a luxury high-rise as it skimmed the capital's skyline, then banked abruptly in the opposite direction, changing course.

The Loach stayed on its tail the entire time. Only Sewell's expertise behind the controls kept them out of the smaller craft's spray of lead death.

"Landmarks, Amy!" Sewell called back to her. "Gimme a landmark, honey! Something I can set my sights on! A fountain, some *Gone with the Wind* columns, a rose garden, maybe a big tamarind tree in

159

the backyard or something — anything so I'll have some idea where it's at. Me and the boys gave this town a real once-over before we set down to look for you! Tell me anything you can remember about the place. It just might register!" The craft tilted to the left and ascended sharply, just as another spray of tracers smoked past on the right. Ross wondered what people on the ground were thinking about the nighttime aerial show. He watched the glowing slugs lose velocity and drop into a sleeping housing project.

"But why?" Amy couldn't grasp all of it yet. "What good will it do?"

Collins slapped her along the edge of the chin, shocking her. "Just tell him, damnit! Everything you can remember! *You wanna live to see the sunrise?*"

"A pool!" she screamed back at Brent, ignoring Sewell and Ross as the sting woke her from her dream — only to welcome her into a nightmare that raced across the rooftops of Manila. "He had a swimming pool in the courtyard!"

"There's swimming pools all across this town!" Ross argued.

"It was huge!" She turned to face the lieutenant. "It was huge and it was in the shape of a woman's curves! You know." And she made the familiar three-sphered figure with her hands.

"Does that help?" Ross yelled up at Sewell, his and the voice of the others in the cabin fighting to be heard above the grinding twist of rotor pitch.

"And there was a statue!" Amy cut in, laughing almost hysterically now as she recalled more and more about the villa.

"A statue?" Sewell glanced back at her as he brought

160

the chopper through another series of death-defying maneuvers mere feet above a dizzying maze of twelfth floor rooftops.

"It must have been twenty feet high!" she dropped off into an embarrassed giggle which couldn't be heard but the others watched her hand come up to cover her grinning teeth. It was an Oriental custom that angered Sewell. And intrigued Ross. Collins had never noticed, despite his police training in the art of observation.

"Twenty feet high?" Brent pushed his nose up against hers and brushed her hand aside as the helicopter rolled over onto its side again, threatening to drop them all out into space — but somehow they remained unmoving, "glued" to the spot. "*What* the hell was twenty feet high?" he screamed, shaking her by the shoulders.

"*A fucking erect penis!*" She matched his glare, refusing to back down. "A giant, fucking Japanese prick!" Amy flashed him an evil, satisfied smile and licked her lower lip. "He had it brought over all the way from Tokyo!"

"Some of the Japs worship phallic symbols," Sewell turned and told Ross matter-of-factly, as if they were not right then flying in and out of leaning tenements at one-hundred-plus miles per hour. "Saw 'em all over the hills north of Tokyo. Five, ten, fifteen feet high! Some as big as hot-air balloons! I tell ya, Roscoe, *them* Asians are not one to be outdone when it comes to preservin' the family jewels! Hell, I never *seen* such a sight before!"

"Sounds like my kind of people!" Ross ducked to the left unnecessarily as a spray of tracers came uncomfortably close, then veered off into the night, away from their craft. "But I don't remember no giant

161

whangers bein' worshipped anywhere around here."

Collins was about to remark about the startled masseuse he and Matt had lined up the night before they found Amy, when the chopper suddenly dropped several feet and bucked to the side. A deafening thump—like a sledge hammer slamming against a barrel—had immediately preceded the loss of power. "We been hit!" he yelled instead.

"Just a round in the tail boom!" Sewell assured him. "Nothing to worry about—got it back under control. Happened all the time back during my old MASH days pullin' grunts out o' the Korean muck!"

"And an old plane!" Amy pushed herself up from the floor of the cabin. "He had this old bi-plane mounted in the rear courtyard! I don't think it ever even flew, but he had it all fixed up—painted white and black like a Zebra, with red Japanese circles on the wings."

"Rising sun emblems," Collins decided, though he was no student of Japanese culture.

Ross and Sewell exchanged knowing looks. Matt nodded eagerly. "You thinkin' about the place I'm thinkin' about, flyboy?"

"The description bangs a gong in the old belfry, Roscoe!" Sewell changed course, banking sharply to the right. "The description definitely bangs an ever-loving gong!"

The Loach stayed on their tail for the next several minutes, unleashing scattered blasts of mini-gun and cannon fire, but not a single direct hit was scored by the airborne prison guards.

"Aren't they ever gonna run out of fuel?" Collins complained as Sewell took them through another gauntlet of evasive maneuvers, designed to tear apart weak stomachs. "I thought you dudes put their tanks out of commission before effecting the great escape?" His words were sarcasm-laced.

"They must have switched to a reserve tank we didn't see!" Sewell replied as they missed a rooftop by inches. The chopper's downblast sent umbrellas poolside flying over the edge to the street several flights below.

"Lousy Loaches don't have no reserve tanks!" he argued.

"Everything that flies has a reserve tank, mister rocket scientist," Matt replied dryly. Ross decided Collins never heard him, but then they were diving down between lancelike buildings of white and gray again, and everyone's stomachs were in their throats for the mandatory eight-second count.

"What's the plan, gents?" Collins screamed up to the crazy man behind the controls at the same time Ross asked, "Do you see it?"

"That's the protruding pecker!" Sewell ignored Collins as he pointed down at the distant statue, bathed in bright lights of alternating white and purple.

"Yep!" Amy drew closer to the cockpit for a better look as the Dragonfly began its steep descent toward the target two thousand feet away. "I'd recognize that hard-on from a mile off, anyday!"

Ross laughed out loud, the force of the dive drawing his cheeks back as he clapped his grinning chopper pilot on the shoulder. "Do your thing, flyboy. I just hope the madman on our tail wants us bad enough to keep kissin' our ass all the way down!"

"And *I* just hope that asshole's five daughters are home at this hour!" Amy's eyes focused on the gallery-like villa set into the hillside in front of the plaster penis rising up through the mist. The tri-level building was ringed with security lights, positioned along the glass-shard-topped brick fence, that shone down through the dreamy haze, casting a surrealistic glow across the compound. Lights inside the light-brown teakwood structure burned dimly—but from this altitude, the war dogs could not make out any people inside.

"Ready to take her down?" Ross yelled across at Sewell.

"Eleven hundred feet!" the chopper pilot answered with a shifting of the foot controls. "Minus *ten* hundred feet and counting!"

"Say your prayers, baby!" Collins called across the cabin to Amy.

"I ain't talked to the Big Boy in a couple lifetimes, honey!" She was now busy chewing a slice of bubble-gum Ross had slipped her after they became airborne. Amy chewed bubblegum viciously, especially at times like this—until the tight lips made it look like an act of violence.

"And I doubt if He'd listen to her if she did!" Sewell called back over her shoulder as the helicopter gained speed and the synchronized elevator in the tail of the craft began to whine. "Seven hundred feet, ladies!"

"Get all sharp objects out of your pockets!" Ross was suddenly yelling insanely—his brand of humor—as he imitated a wall poster he had seen hanging in Mimi's Bar back in Saigon. "Tuck your head down between your legs—"

"And kiss your ass goodbye!" Collins had seen the same poster.

Sewell's grin brightened. They were both referring to a farcical sign someone had posted in the event the Thinktank down in the War Room elected to ever nuke Vietnam and start all over. From scratch. But death was death, he decided. Be it an atomic explosion or a fiery helicopter crash. The way the ground was rapidly rising up to meet them, both would be just about as instantaneous. And devastating.

"Hold on!" Matt the madman's jaw jutted across toward Ross and the others while his eyes remained on the skyline of buildings rushing up at them. "Here goes nothing!"

In less than a breath's gasp, the craft looped upward and began a sudden ascent that nearly sheared the rotors off. The Loach might have been capable of an identical maneuver, but the pilot was not so experienced — it slammed into the villa beside the glowing phallic symbol and exploded in a magnificent fireball that rolled out across the compound, consuming everything in its path.

Including the plaster erection that towered over the collapsed and crackling bi-plane.

Sewell circled over the burning villa a couple times, and they watched guards on the ground trying to enter the building to search for survivors, only to be driven back by the heat. Bursting propane tanks sent secondary explosions of bright pink-and-green fireballs climbing the skyline, and Ross finally directed Sewell to take them back to Cebu where they could refuel prior to leaving for South Vietnam, five hundred miles away.

"Such a waste," Amy mused as she watched the walls of ringing flame engulf the Japanese work of art. Now that they were back at cruising speed, conversation did not have to be shouted back and forth as loudly. "Such a waste."

"That would have been a real ball-buster, baby." Collins flashed her an evil, challenging grin. "Even for a . . . *lady* of your considerable talents and expertise. I mean, I was almost afraid you were gonna reach out and try to grab hold o' that humongous cock back there! I saw the hungry gleam in your eyes!" he taunted her. "It would have been the ultimate challenge, right?" He ducked back as she sent a playful swing his way. "Trying to swallow a twenty-foot—"

Amy lunged at him, got the ex-policeman in a headlock, and flipped him onto his back as the helicopter flop-flop-flopped up into the thick, ominous cloud cover. "I give!" Collins gasped as she increased pressure on his windpipe. "I give up! Uncle! *Uncle!*"

"No way, sucker!" she screamed with satisfaction— loud enough so the others in the smoothly vibrating craft could hear. "Not till you lick my asshole clean, boy!"

"I love that kind of talk!" Sewell nodded back over a shoulder to Ross. Neither man had any idea what set off the two this time.

"Reminds me of the time the *canh-sats* back in Saigon arrested one of their meter maids after a background check showed she was once a hooker with documented sympathies toward the VC. I ever tell you this one?"

"Coupla times." Sewell leveled off just above the lowest layer of piled-up cumulus and followed a meandering valley of dull white southward. Castlelike formations rose up on both sides of the helicopter. *Cory would love it*, Sewell decided as the sweat between his fingers began to soak into the flight gloves. *Just like the Greek gods guarding Zeus's kingdom over earth.* He glanced about the craft again, feeling suddenly uneasy as the glowing walls seemed to close in on them. *Or just like dragons.*

"Anyway," Ross continued, "so they take the bitch up for a little truth or consequences—get my drift? And she kinda 'accidentally' stumbles out the back door of the chopper at two thousand feet."

Sewell held his nose closed. "Ooooow, Roscoe. El grosso, man! You tryin' to bum me out or something?"

"I don't know if she was flappin' her arms home or what, but damned if she don't land right in front of the Continental Hotel, her home turf." He paused just the right amount of time between locations. "Legs spread wide, smack *dab* on a parkin' meter, son!"

"A parking meter?" Sewell glanced back at his lieutenant, feigning intense disbelief, just like always. (Except that before, they were usually well along in the advanced stages of intoxication in some Tu Do Street bar.)

"A parking meter!" Ross affirmed. "Legs spread wide, landed smack *dab* on a fucking parking meter."

"Oh, now you've done it, Roscoe!" Sewell was a good actor. He looked like he was about to blow his oats right then and there. "Now you've really gone and done it! I'm gonna puke all over the instrument panel!" He calmly set his sights on the horizon, and their stepping stones back to the Nam. "I swear I'm about to lose it, boss man *and it's all gonna be your lousy fault!*" The words left him like they had practiced them time and time again.

Behind the two soldiers, Amy and Brent continued

167

wrestling across the belly of the cabin, ignoring the pilot and his partner — concentrating only on the way their limbs tangled together at just the right angles as they too put on the usual show.

"Took 'em three hours for the ambulance crew to pluck her off that parking meter, Matt, my boy!" Ross continued, running a fingernail against the crack between two front teeth.

"Ohhhhhh, ughhhh," Sewell groaned believably.

"And ten days for the undertaker to get the smile off her face."

11

Saigon

Things did not feel right to April Adams. Her head felt elevated several feet above the rest of her body, and her reflexes felt sluggish — though, even from this height, her limbs seemed to be swaying just right to the beat of the music.

The music. So moody. Soft and seductive — like her tight, thigh-riding outfit — yet frightening. Cigarette smoke, thick and billowing, floated from table to table below her. Blue mist between the bobbing heads and shifting eyes. Someone dropped another coin in the juke box, and the same Moody Blues song oozed forth from the giant wall speakers, over and over.

But she could not remember the name.

She glanced across the room. Another girl was also dancing for the loud and drunk patrons of the night-club, but they had her in some kind of cage suspended from a thick beam running across the ceiling. Flashing lights encircled the cage. It almost looked like a bamboo cage, but somehow she knew it was made of metal.

The crowd was yelling up at the girl. She was dancing much too fast for the music. Her hips gyrated about madly and she made her chest flop up and down with each drum beat, generating even more cheers. And then her skirt flew from a raised leg that was kicking wildly back and forth, and all she wore was a bikini bottom that rode the crack of her haunches and couldn't even be seen in the rear.

April glanced down at her arms as she fought to concentrate more on her dancing. She was finally on her pedestal, turning on the people, showing them her skill. But they still wouldn't let her sing, and the marks on her wrists were really starting to bother her. Though, suspended so far above her shoulders as her mind was, it was hard to really care that much. And she hadn't been irritated at the manager for nights. Even after she had awakened beneath his booze-bloated body for the second morning in a row.

Her eyes drifted to the ends of her long fingernails— coated with blood-red polish that had gold flecks in it—and beyond: to the brown bamboo bars rising up all around her. The brown bamboo bars that were really metal.

She couldn't remember how she got inside the cage. All she could remember was that they had finally let her out of the room. That they had finally let her dance.

"Why don't *you* show some skin, baby!" A fifty-year-old GI was reaching up and pawing her, trying to stuff a ten-dollar bill into her panties. A bouncer appeared out of nowhere, and the customer — his accent sounded more Aussie than American — was politely persuaded back into his chair.

"Do what they ask!" the bouncer, a broad-shouldered Vietnamese with a long mustache and narrow, suspicious eyes, snapped before turning his back on her.

April pursed her lips distastefully and swung herself around so she wouldn't have to look at the sex-starved soldiers, just in from the field. The face that greeted her in the mirrored wall — her own — startled her into frozen helplessness. Were the eyes really hers? Those dazed, sunken orbs — were they really attached to a body that felt so free, so in tune with the cosmos?

As she stared into the unblinking eyes, April felt herself floating back down into her body. She felt herself being drawn back into reality by her own reflection. The heroin-induced stupor was ebbing, her limbs were becoming more awkward, more non-responsive.

"Take it off, honey!" Another soldier had waited until the bouncer disappeared beyond the endless wall of tables before reaching up to grab her buttocks. She could not feel his hand, but she could see what he was doing, and she made a feeble attempt to swat out at him.

Her ears heard his table erupt into laughter when she missed, and the swing took her off balance. Her sexy high heels tilted to the side precariously for a moment, then she collapsed.

171

A gasp went up from several surrounding tables as her cage swung from side to side with the momentum, and a hush fell across half the bar until one of the floor managers sent a loud, racy song through the juke box speakers and April was hustled off into a back room.

She awoke with her panties dangling from one ankle and a strange man across her, slamming his pelvis against hers violently. Her legs felt spread to their limits, yet he was pushing them apart even farther, until she was sure the skin inside her thighs would split. His rough, callused hands were squeezing her breasts together as he sucked on one then the other, back and forth with each plunge, but she felt powerless to resist, totally drained of energy.

So she just lay there. For endless periods of time. While he grunted and groaned against her ear, twisted her body about to suit his pleasure, then finally exploded deep inside her and collapsed across her chest, breathing hard.

Long after he drifted off to sleep, still atop her, sprawled across her, April found her hand moving up his back from the hips. Her fingers explored the smooth folds of skin at the base of his skull—though she could still not really feel anything—and slid up across the top of it. And now she felt it to be smooth as a baby's bottom. Shaved. Visions of Bullethead drifted into her consciousness.

It was Cotton. Again.

She closed her eyes and drifted back down into the dark pit where it was frightening but she had come to feel safe. She did not even feel when he pulled out of her. When he rolled her onto her stomach and punctured the skin of her inner thigh and then her wrist with another syringe.

When her eyes opened, she was standing in the bamboo cage again, wearing a different miniskirt this time, and a new set of undergarments, but the same carefree expression. Or so it seemed.

She didn't turn to look in the mirrored wall anymore. She didn't want to see the face. The sunken eyes of the ghost from her past.

So she stared down at the drunken bar customers instead. And she smiled seductively at their suggestive proposals and probing hands as they strained on tiptoes to cop a feel when the bouncers weren't looking.

She was amazed at how well she had adjusted to the seamy nightclub environment, at how skillfully she was dancing. In her head, she sang along with the words from the songs blaring from the juke box speakers—and she truly felt her voice sounded better than the singers some record company in New York or Hollyweird was paying ridiculous millions to—but her singing was no longer of prime importance in her life. Even the dancing was becoming just another hindrance, though she hadn't felt her limbs moving in weeks.

All that mattered anymore were the infrequent sessions with Cotton. And the magic juice he shot into her veins.

She had fallen in love with the man with the bullet head.

* * *

"It's gonna be a hot one!" the door gunner screamed above the roar of flapping rotors as the gunship skimmed a few inches above the shimmering sea of elephant grass. "I can taste it in the air, gents! Gonna be a might hot LZ! Zip up the ol' flak jackets and don't forget the Chrissy medals."

Plumes of restless purple smoke spiraling up from a clearing at the edge of the rain forest became suddenly visible in the distance. " 'Cause it's gonna be a hotter 'an hell LZ!" the door gunner raved on, teeth flashing as bone-white knuckles gripped the handles of the Hog-60. In the background, metallic voices crackled across the radio net. Frantic voices. American voices, calling for help: more grunts, more ammo. And medevac slicks. *Lotsa Dustoffs!*

Big Chad Chandler braced the M-1 carbine against his belly and leaped off after the last of the Air Cavalry soldiers. Behind him the reporter with the notorious reputation, Darnette, followed with unsure footing as the rice-paddy foliage swallowed him up to the hips. Leg muscles pumped furiously as boots sucked through the muck.

"Keep your head down!" Chandler called back to him as they struggled to catch up to the rock-hard grunts rapidly vanishing in the walls of drifting gun smoke. Lead zinged in all around them from Viet Cong snipers scattered in the tree tops. On either side of their chopper, more aircraft were setting down, until nearly a dozen Hueys had landed. The combined downblasts of all their rotors flattened the sharp reeds against the soggy earth. The air became one loud, solid, chopping vibration as the gunships idled momentarily, then ascended back up through the ground-clinging mist to make room for more.

Operation Valiant Hawk was getting into full swing. Designed to surround a battalion-sized cluster of tunnel VC in their Mekong Delta stronghold with a surprise four-pronged attack, the mission had already run into full-scale resistance. Both sides were taking heavy casualties.

"This is great!" Chandler called up to a nineteen-year-old lieutenant who had offered them a ride south into the Delta, where action was brewing in a never-ending cycle and death was put on hold. "I eat this shit up!"

Behind them, Darnette tripped and stumbled over his camera gear, cursing loudly—totally ignoring, it seemed, the clods of dislodged dirt ricocheting all around his feet. "Fucking Mytho," he muttered under his breath. "Always the same can o' worms. Why can't I ever get a hop up to Pleiku anymore?"

"What's his problem?" the baby-faced officer yelled over to Chad as they dove behind a pile of bodies moments before a sheet of shrapnel swirled past like a monsoon downpour.

"Aw, he's never happy unless he's moanin' and groanin'," the ex-mercenary almost laughed. "You know the type—fucking foreign correspondents! Always got their heads and their ego up their rectal cavity!"

Chandler's smile faded when he noticed the name tag on the uniform shielding him was in English and not Vietnamese. He had refused to stare at the faces a couple feet away, but America's involvement in Indochina was suddenly coming into sharp focus.

"Just met the clown in a bar yesterday, actually!" The excuse flowed out freely, but Chandler's jaw dropped when he glanced back at the lieutenant. The man's face was missing. Only a red slash of gnarled flesh remained above the lower jaw. He had not even heard the round hit the kid. "Aw, fuck," he groaned, wondering when he would ever get used to what he saw on battlefields across the globe. He pushed the trembling body away. "Bet the kid was still a cherry-boy, too."

A huge lizard scurried across Chandler's leg, and he sucked his breath in as it frantically scrambled up over the pile of bodies and charged boldly into battle. "Jesus!"

When no scales were blown back at him, he let the air out and grabbed the lieutenant's Thompson .45 machine gun.

The ground shuddered slightly beside him and he turned to see Darnette dive against the human hill of dripping crimson.

"Greetings and solicitations," the reporter said sarcastically, bringing up one of his cameras to attach a telephoto lens to it. "Welcome to the front."

"There is no front in the Nam," Chandler said dryly. "I figured you knew that by now."

Mortars whistled down onto the hills to their left, and they hugged the earth as shrapnel flew inches above their heads.

"Just a manner of speech," Darnette replied, brushing dirt from his hair. He had lost the bush hat Chandler saw him wearing on the chopper during the flight in. His TV suit (the kind of tailored khakis that made one appear he was about to embark on a safari) was drenched in sweat. "This whole war's just a clusterfuck of words and culture shock."

"Kinda like 'No man in a foxhole under siege is an atheist,' right?" Chandler yelled above the roar of a gunship passing a few feet overhead. He was not sure why he said that.

"Religion is the root of all wars, really," Darnette screamed back. "I don't care what anybody says. That's what forms and separates nations — it's not land. It's not fortunes in gold, though some historians would have you believe that. Look at the world today, mate! Everywhere: nothing but holy wars."

"I wouldn't really call this a holy war," Chandler argued.

A huge Chinook helicopter descended from the advancing wall of storm clouds and hovered over an area less than a football field from the line of U.S. soldiers. Its dual set of powerful rotors whipping up dust and pieces of reeds, three bright beams of smoky red light shot down from its belly and began crisscrossing the tangled terrain. Tracers.

"Beautiful!" Darnette rose to one knee and began filming the show as men groaned in pain only yards away. "This oughta piss off that hotdog squad of stringers from KL I been competin' with all month!"

What am I doing here? Chandler wondered as another VC mortar slammed into the race stalks to his left. Even as the thought bounced about in his head, shook silly by the rolling concussions, the former paratrooper was peppering the men in black pajamas running through the distant treeline with his carbine, and he knew why he had set aside a day away from Zemm to return to the jungle and the carnage that lay in wait there. Death always gave new meaning to his life. Engaging in combat and surviving to fight another day supplied a sense of job satisfaction his long, hot days guarding some rich slob's cattle on the African plains could never afford.

As if every soldier on that small stretch of Asian earth sensed impending doom, the sporadic riflefire grew to a deafening crescendo, then abruptly ceased, leaving a tense, shifting silence across the land. Storm clouds raced past overhead, sending shadows pouring through the rice paddies, and a warm pounding sheet of rainfall swept across the blank, blackened faces of the men without warning.

"That's it!" a middle-aged buck sergeant with a gray crew cut and sweat-lined biceps urged his men forward. "Sweep the joint up, *girls*! Let's move it!' Blood trickled down from a minor shrapnel wound to his cheek. "And don't nobody go walkin' into a set of whirlybird rotors! No sick leave available today! Keep your eyes open! Beat feet but no retreat—keep it neat! *I wanna see some meat!* Cold, dead meat from the bad, bad Victor Charlie! Now double-time it!"

Chandler swallowed as he listened to the career NCO. The man was floating on an adrenaline high, no doubt about that, but he had never heard of the combat rush making soldiers semi-poetic when it came to firing directives at their troopers.

Big Chad and Darnette followed the last wave of injured stragglers and walking wounded up to a paddy dike berm that was full of booby-trapped spider holes: push the webs aside and you had a narrow tunnel entrance. Narrow for round-eyed grunts, but not Charlie.

Mangled bodies of several dozen guerrillas floated in the paddy water below.

Behind them, a fleet of medevac slicks was swooping in to pick up wounded soldiers. "Took forty W.I.A. this trip," Chandler overheard a medic report to a battle-weary platoon leader. "These berms are full of supply line tunnels," another short-timer remarked. "Never saw anything like it. I didn't think you could build an underground cache in the delta!"

Overhead, like a mothership, the Chinook flew tight circles around the scene, guarding its children, while smaller Cobra gunships, sleek and deadly, hovered half in and out of the drifting mist, painted teeth along their vicious-looking snouts grinning in anticipation of more quick kills. Their mixed light and dark green camouflaged paint scheme inspired Chandler to a state of near-arousal—they were floating death, waiting to pounce. Looking menacing as metal monsters as they hung suspended in the sky, waiting and watching, Big Chad felt they were, next to a charging rogue elephant, the most ominous sight he had ever seen. Beside Chandler, the reporter was snapping off pictures left and right. "Great stuff!" he claimed confidently. "Six o'clock network news material, in fact. *No lie, GI!*"

Two soldiers were rushing from body to body along the high paddy dike, seizing weapons. Chandler could not see one guerrilla who had been unarmed at the time of his death. He glanced over at Darnette. The man seemed obsessed with photographing the circling Chinook from every possible angle on the ground. He took pictures of the dead VC too, but most shots were made *after* the AK-47s and SKSs were dragged away, and that struck him as odd.

Two soldiers erected an American flag on a long bamboo pole, and a smaller, gold Vietnamese flag, with its three horizontal red stripes flapping in the breeze, and as the elusive symbols of freedom and security in Southeast Asia flew from the highest point along the crumbling berm, Chandler whipped an informal salute at them. "Old Glory standing strong amidst settling gun smoke," he sighed loud enough for Darnette to hear. "Kinda makes you proud, don't it?" But the reporter only spat at the ground, as if bothered by all the patriotic emotions that always accompanied flag waving and, staring down at his camera, grumbled something about old film.

"Found a rice cache over there." The buck sergeant, sporting a stubby cigar along the edge of his lower lip now, appeared in front of Darnette, eager to assist the reporter in immortalizing his Air Cav unit. "My guys are about to torch it."

"Torch it?" A demonic grin crept across Darnette's bone-clinging features.

"Yeah. We used to piss on the piles of rice, or shovel shit into the middle of 'em and just leave it at that, but somebody armchair-quarterbacking back at Puzzle Palace concluded such was not gentlemanly behavior. So now we burn it all to the ground." The sergeant waved his hands back and forth in front of his face casually and a cloud of mosquitoes that had floated up on the warm breeze dispersed in a swirl of frenzied activity.

Darnette glanced over at a decapitated Viet Cong and frowned at the buzzing flies congregating on the open throat wound. What appeared to be black, clotting blood was really a shifting blanket of the large, hungry pests that flew away from the corpse now and then to inspect the faces of the dazed men standing around. "What about villagers?" He watched the American teen-agers with carbines slung over their shoulders upside-down touch Zippo cigarette lighters with "Sorry 'Bout That, Victor Charlie" and outline maps of Indochina inscribed on them to the straw hut containing gunny sacks of rice and a crate of Chicom stick grenades. As the fire started to crackle, silver smoke fanned out to engulf the GIs and the shredded bodies at their feet.

"Villagers?" The veteran NCO grinned incredulously.

"Yeah. Women, children?"

"Not at these numbers, sir," he laughed. "This is just a VC supply depot. Totally military, though Charlie *is* notorious for building his sanctuaries in the midst of civilian population centers. But this here's totally military. No kids. No cunts."

"Though we could sure use a little R&R right about now," a seventeen-year-old machine gunner standing behind the sergeant blushed bashfully, and Chandler wondered if a red face could be feigned—he had never tried it before. The kid stood with his feet braced apart and the weight of the M-60 as a balance to counteract his bent knees. Big Chad wondered what the youth's high-school classmates were doing back in The World right then, or if he had even graduated. And how many were buried in the red clay of Vietnam? How many had died right on this steaming delta battlefield? The trooper reminded him of Cory, back in Saigon.

"No kids. No cunts." The sergeant bit the cigar stub in half and spit it out. It plopped into the paddy water with a nauseating splash that sent gas expanding in Chandler's stomach. "Nothing but stale rice and a whole dumptruck load of stinkin' dinks. Forty-seven KIA's the body count so far, if you wanna include those stats in your story. You can quote me." He pointed at the blood-splattered name tag on his chest. "That's Nunez, sir. Nunez with a 'Z.'"

Darnette mumbled something unintelligible under his breath, brushed past the sergeant and began zooming in on the burning hut with his telephoto lens. Flames leaped a dozen feet into the air now, driving off a horde of gnats that had drifted in toward the paddy, drawn by the stench of blood pools collecting at the water's edge.

"That dude gives off bad vibes," the sergeant whispered to Chandler moments later. "I don't know what it is, but I almost get the feeling he's working for the other side. What was his name, sir?" He focused on Chandler's name tag, which read BRAZES.

"Darnette, Sarge." The "sir" had made Big Chad flinch, but he understood the reason for it. Some career soldiers addressed all civilians, even news media types clad in fatigues, with it, out of some sense of misplaced respect. Chandler felt it should be the other way around. Nine-to-five high-rise executives in New York, or L.A. were raking in hundreds of thousands a year because of weapons sales to Indochina, yet an infantryman walking point in a mist-cloaked Asian jungle could count on less than a lousy hundred a month for doing what Big Chad considered the most dangerous job in the world. And the C-note—before Uncle Sammy's taxes—arrived only if you survived the *body* count!

The tired NCO's grim smile faded. "Darnette? Darnette the freelancin' freeloader?"

"Same-same, I guess."

A couple enlisted men were gathering around the sergeant as another helicopter floated in behind them. "Darnette?" one whispered to the other in an irritated tone.

"Yeah, I think that's what I heard."

"Well, fuck us all then. He hasn't gotten a story straight since he covered that Cho Gao affair last year."

"Since he set foot in the Nam," his brush partner agreed.

"*You!*" The sergeant pointed at Darnette. "Out o' my AO, sleazebucket." His arm swung around toward the Huey, upon which the wounded were rapidly being loaded. The dead were slowly going into vomit-green body bags with fiberglass zippers. They were in no hurry to leave. "I want you on the first bird out! And no arguments about your First Amendment rights! I'll ram the fuckin' Constitution up your ass, mister!" The sergeant's hand rested on the butt of his holstered automatic. He was pissed. And he meant business. Jungle justice was swift and deadly. It could apply to a rip-off reporter just as well as anybody else.

Darnette shrugged his shoulders like he'd heard it all a hundred times before. "OK, awright, sergeant sir." Walking backwards casually, he continued clicking off photos all the way up to the Huey's dust-coated skids. "Don't get your tit in a wringer!"

"Oughta bury 'im neck-deep in the berm," Chandler overheard one grunt telling another. "Let the fire ants get to his asshole and *then* see how quick his pucker factor adopts to the true scheme of things here in the good ol' RVN."

"The dude do definitely have an attitude problem," someone else remarked as hostile glares were exchanged between soldier and civilian. "Duty on an anthill LP would certainly change his commie-sympathizer approach to covering the conflict here."

"Conflict?" A forty-year-old corporal erupted from his post-battle silence, fueling a separate argument.

"Nothin' can change 'em, Ricky," the shorter of the two privates cut in, forcing the E-4 back into his shocked shell. The PFC began wiping powder residue from his rifle's flash suppressor with an o.d. green handkerchief. "They're all born with Russian-red enemas up their yin-yang."

"You lovelies take it easy now, hear?" Darnette stumbled over several wounded soldiers as he climbed into the chopper, intent on claiming the canvas butt strap farthest from the open hatch and exposure to stray rounds from the ground or tree tops. "Oughta have you all on the front page of the *Vietnam Guardian* by sunup tomorrow! Don't forget to stop by your local hamlet newspaper stand on your way out to the next hill hump!"

"Fucking maggot," one soldier muttered as the Huey's idling rotors changed pitch and began picking up speed. A cool but dirty breeze rushed out to touch the men.

Before the chopper lifted off, however, a twelve-year-old Vietnamese girl wearing only black silk pajama bottoms and a straw, conical hat emerged from the treeline and rushed up to one of the nearby slicks. Despite the innocent look on her face, every grunt watching spotted the telltale signs of determination in her rapid gait.

Before she was halfway across the rice paddy, a dozen carbines were trained on her undeveloped chest.

Seconds later, her back exploded with a sickly red spray and the satchel charge she had been carrying detonated, tearing her torso in half at the waist. The top flopped down beside several Americans who were lying in the ankle-deep water already wounded and being attended by medics, and the secondary explosion killed four of them and blinded one of the corpsman.

"My God . . ." The words escaped Chandler as he watched a squad of men run over to assist their brother soldiers. Two gunships converged on the meandering treeline and showered it with tracers until not a single palm frond remained intact. Naked trunks protruded from the ground-clinging smoke awkwardly, trembling from the rain of lead.

A third Cobra circled the kill zone, its nose dipping down diagonally and trained on the center of the paddy forty feet below while its tail boom followed the arc lazily.

Chandler watched Darnette crowd the open hatch of his chopper, hurriedly recording the unfolding drama with his trusty telephoto lens, and then the Huey began rising amidst a cloud of dust and twigs. The reporter was directing a thumbs-up gesture at him suddenly.

Big Chad couldn't, for the life of him, imagine why.

12

Tu Do Street, Saigon

A freezing mist clouded the edges of the out-of-focus scene unfolding in front of her.

The man was fifty yards away, arms outstretched, screaming her name as he ran toward her, blood spurting from a sucking chest wound with each footfall.

In the distance, a dozen Chinese soldiers were chasing him, firing their rifles on the run.

Her arms went out to him—she could see the fingertips rising through the mist in front of her—but before they embraced, the man vanished in a shower of blood. It was as if a trap door had suddenly opened up beneath his feet. . . .

April Adams sat up in bed as if a sledge hammer had just come down across her stomach. The word "Father!" was still echoing in her ears. Her short, purple nighty was drenched in sweat.

She glanced about the small, barren cubicle that had been her room for the last two weeks, well aware she had just woken from another nightmare. But she felt she was not alone.

The room was dark except for a soft glow of blue and green neon flashing off and on outside the barred window. Juke box music on the other side of one wall sent the wood to vibrating with each drumbeat.

A hand grabbed her wrist, and April screamed—but the sound was drowned out by sudden laughter in the hallway outside.

"Shut up, bitch!" a husky voice boomed into one ear and the back of a hairy hand slapped her out of the bed onto the floor. "Got a paying customer for you to *entertain*."

The bolt on the outside of the door slid back with a harsh grating sound and a sixty-year-old Japanese businessman staggered through the narrow frame, drunk. In the smoky light that filtered in, April could see an armed guard with one hand on the doorknob. Behind him, people were laughing and drinking at the tables below the stairwell that led up to the open second-floor corridor of small "sleeping booths." The dance floor was elbow-to-elbow Vietnamese bargirls and American GIs.

Before the door slammed shut, she saw Cotton's bullet-smooth crown gleaming in the neon glow pulsing through the window. Then she was alone with the two men.

The customer grunted an insincere greeting in Japanese. He reached out and pressed his right hand against her breast boldly, pushing the flesh as flat as it would go.

April swung a wide, sidearmed pitch at him, and though her aim was uncoordinated and sluggish, the fist connected with the businessman's nose and he staggered backwards, off balance.

Cotton lashed out and slammed a fist against her cheek, and April dropped to the floor, stunned. Tears filled her eyes.

"Now that's no way to treat our friend, Mr. Nissan here!" He reached down and grabbed her nighty at the waist and ripped it away with one rough jerk. "You know our slogan here is, 'The customer's always Numba One!' "

He dropped to one knee beside her and spread her legs apart with his hands. "Dig in, emperor!" He smiled up at the businessman. "Per your request: white meat!"

Nissan shook his head from side to side, frowning. "No good!" He sounded adamant. "No good you watch."

"No, no, no!" Cotton's teeth flashed brightly in the dim light. "I just help you make the plunge, papa-san. Got you a real feisty fighter here. Thought you might need a little *assist*. Now go ahead: drop your drawers and take the dive. *Banzai!*"

"*Banzai?*" The man belched loudly, wavered from side to side and clasped his hands as if preparing to attempt a swan dive from a high cliff into shallow waters by torchlight. "*Banzai?*"

"*Banzai!*" Cotton shifted around behind April and held her down by the shoulders, though she was weak and hardly resisting as it was—the drugs had drained her willpower and sapped her strength weeks before. With his chin, Cotton motioned toward the open thighs beckoning the stranger.

"No . . . *Cotton*," April whimpered softly, shaking her head from side to side, humiliated and insulted, hurt.

189

"Why? Why are you making me do these things? I feel so — so — dirty."

A smile slowly crept across Nissan's face as he spotted the moist folds of pink skin below the bushy mound. He began fumbling with his belt.

"No!" April called out, her voice a scream finally. "Let me up! Don't do this to me, Cotton! How can you do this to me? *I love you!*"

"Shut up!" the Bulletman snapped, fingers digging into her bare shoulders. "Or I'll sell you to that Arab motherfucker forming a handjob harem down on Thong Nhut."

As the Japanese dropped to his knees, still swaying from side to side, April closed her eyes tightly and thought about the man in her nightmares. *Please come to me now!* she prayed. *Please save me from this!*

Nissan tumbled against her just as the face appeared in her mind. He forced himself into her with such force she cried out in shock. Her haunches slid across the smooth teakwood floor as he gained a foothold against one wall and thrust into her violently. With her head against the corner partition, neck bent, April retreated deeper and deeper into her mental fortress of solitude until she felt herself falling into the terrible black pit.

The man's grunts and groans slowly faded away until they were a mere distorted echo of the hell she had been suffering only moments ago.

When she opened her eyes, April was in the bamboo cage again, dancing for the howling GIs below. She had no idea how she got there, where the Japanese bastard was now, or who had bathed and dressed her.

Her left arm smarted, and she glanced down at a

190

black line running along the wrist someone had tried to conceal with flesh-toned makeup. She did not know this signalled a collapsed vein. She did not know what Cotton was doing to her, though faint voices were constantly trying to tell her little things. Her mind hadn't functioned properly in a dozen days.

A black soldier with a billowing afro that stretched far beyond regulation length reached up and grabbed her ankle through the metal bars painted to look like bamboo, and she slipped and fell to the hard floor of the suspended cage. Harsh words were exchanged at the tables below, and a fight broke out. But only a few seconds passed before a shrill whistle cut through the din and the brawlers scurried for the exits; an MP foot beat passing by had stopped to investigate the crash of breaking beer bottles.

She locked eyes with one of the young, freckled military policemen, but he cast her a disgusted scowl and glanced back down at his clipboard without ever catching the pleading, desperate expression on her face.

Two other MPs were scuffling with a drunk on the floor in front of him, trying to handcuff the man behind the back despite arms the size of tree trunks, but he did not feel the need to scuff up his spitshine by helping them just yet.

Five minutes later, all the black helmets were gone. The assisting patrol jeeps outside pulled away, en route to a backlog of pending bar fights and shots-fired reports.

April knew her body was still moving fluidly to the slow beat of the music. The tune playing just then was one of her favorites — from where or when she couldn't remember, but the man's voice made her feel good, whatever feelings she had left, and brought forth blurred memories of her youth. . . .

She saw herself playing in a colorful garden, bright collages of flowers all around—a tiny poodle in her lap, licking her chin. And behind the little girl stood a tall man, his face a silver blank, arms folded across his chest. . . .

Laughter in the distance brought April back to the present and she glanced up to see two American men enter the nightclub, Vietnamese women on their arms. She did not feel the slight smile creep across her lips— the smile of happiness for them. Somehow she realized the girls were not common street whores. They did not even look Vietnamese, actually, but darker. Perhaps Khmer, though she had no firsthand knowledge of skin shades by locale in this part of the world, only what talk she heard from the local dancers in the dressing room. Like the constant reminiscing about a Cambodian waitress who had once worked the swing shift till she latched onto a wingnut from Tan Son Nhut who bought her a visa and plane ride back to the Big PX across the pond. These women looked content, protected. Happy. Spoken for—their future secure. She wondered why *she* felt suddenly happy for *them*.

Or was it envy?

As they passed below her bamboo cage, April squatted, swaying from side to side on her sexy high heels, and reached out to the taller, older man with trembling fingers.

Big Chad Chandler slid to a halt on the booze-slick tile. A grin erupted across his face as the firm breasts in their see-through halter top swayed and bounced

192

about inches in front of his nose. Zemm tightened her hold on his arm and frowned, narrow eyes giving the American woman the suspicious and critical once-over.

"Ma'am?" he asked innocently enough, startled by the unexpected confrontation. An Asian woman knew better than to approach a man who already had someone by his side (it could mean her throat, no matter how many people were watching) but he thought even a *bà-mỹ* wouldn't commit such a defiant act after a few months in-country. As she began to speak, Zemm pulled him away toward an empty table that had magically appeared in the crowded nightclub.

"Aw, honey," Chandler complained loudly, glancing back at April's flaring thighs as she stood up again.

Cory MacArthur's eyes were glued to the go-go dancer's waist-length hair. In his mind, he saw her sitting atop him on a penthouse-suite bed somewhere, hair dangling down across his face, its perfumy fragrance tickling his nose as her shoulders swayed from side to side with the erotic background music. Her breasts brushed against his face as she shifted her hips into a more comfortable and accommodating position, and he saw himself licking the brown swirls erect before filling his mouth with them. But then his no-nonsense Khmer sweetheart was jerking him off balance too. Did he read the words *Help me* on her lips, or was it just his imagination?

"Quite a looker," Chandler told Cory later as they popped beer tops off bottles of *ba muoi ba*. He whispered even though neither Zemm nor his girlfriend knew enough English slang to guess at the word's meaning.

Cory glanced over his shoulder at April, giving their

secret away, and Zemm punched Chandler on the arm. The big ex-merc nearly slid off his chair from the force of the impact.

April had resumed dancing again, but her eyes stayed on the two men at the nearest table, a look of anticipation on her face.

Chandler allowed himself a second or two to stare at April. His eyes focused on her chest again before slowly dropping to her calves.

Zemm reached across the table, grabbed his ear and twisted hard. "You like white woman, *Chad*?" Her words arced out at him like heat lightning.

"Huh?" He pulled away, wincing, but she refused to let go.

"You like big boobs? You like thick bush?" Cory's head sank between his shoulders as he sought to hide his growing smile. Maybe she knew more slang than he gave her credit for. Indochinese women were always full of surprises.

Chandler flashed a smile at Cory. "Big boobs? Thick bush? You been teachin' my wife gutter lingo, boy?"

MacArthur shrugged his shoulders and held his hands out, palms up. The woman sitting beside him slammed her elbow into his stomach and he flopped over face-first into a bowl of pretzels.

"You like those Hollywood hips?" Zemm persisted, lips curling into a sadistic grin as she twisted harder, enjoying the pain she was inflicting. "You like the way round-eyed bitch smile at you?"

Cory left his face in the bowl of pretzels so he could keep smiling without risking retribution. He envisioned Zemm wearing black leather hot pants, metal pasties over her nipples and nothing else as she cracked

194

a whip during their lovemaking sessions. The thought contrasted sharply with the quiet, obedient and submissive image he had held of her all these months.

"She wasn't smiling, Zemm," Chandler corrected her.

A brawl broke out at the next table, and a Marine flew backwards through the air, smashing down across their drinks.

"My fucking pretzels!" Cory yelled, rising to his feet with fists raised. A beer bottle followed the jarhead across the room and bounced off Cory's glass chin. The teakwood floorboards shook like piano keys as he collapsed across them.

April Adams stopped dancing even though the music from the wall speakers increased dramatically in volume—the bouncers always turned the sound system up whenever a fight broke out. Her tiny hands clutching the bars of her "cage," she watched the two couples—Big Chad dragging Cory—sidestepping the growing number of combatants.

Chandler would normally have been right in there swinging with the best of them, but tonight he was laying back, acting the casual vet. After propping MacArthur up in a corner a safe distance from all the hostilities, he found a nearby bar stool and sat down on it. He kicked his boots up on one of the few tables still standing and watched Zemm mother-hen her younger cousin back behind the counter beside the shapely Taiwanese bartender.

Two soldiers stumbled past—wrestling on their feet, not dancing—and Chandler reached out and grabbed a newspaper sticking out of a back pocket. A third drunk tripped into his lap, and after pushing the GI off, the war dog propelled him away with a slow, gentle boot.

"Will you check out this shit." He unfolded the copy of that morning's *Saipan Post*. "The grunts down in the delta were on the level about that Darnette sonofabitch," he spoke to Cory as if the kid were actually listening to anything more than bells and cuckoo birds. A chair flew through the air and crashed against the wall behind him, showering his table top with splinters. "Listen to this. That damned Darnette claims the grunts jumpin' off choppers down outside Cho Gao burnt down a whole village because a landing Huey tripped a bamboo pole frag wire a hundred yards away from the nearest hut."

Sirens pulling up outside signalled the MPs or *canhsats* had been called. Cory shook his head from side to side and began to get up and two more fighting Marines rolled over him.

"He claims several unarmed villagers were gunned down attempting to flee the ensuing carnage!" Chandler continued. He threw the newspaper at Cory, who had just succeeded in pushing the two Marines away. "Check out the picture on his front page story, Mac! It's the little girl the soldiers were forced to kill—but there's no mention made about the explosives she was carrying toward the Americans! Just that bleeding-heart caption: 'Search and Destroy has come to mean SAD.'" He spoke the last eight words with intense sarcasm and not the least bit of skepticism. "I mean *where does this guy get off spouting these lies in print like this?*"

"There oughta be a law," Cory mumbled back at him stupidly, his words running together and his eyes still seeing spots and stars. But he wasn't looking at Big

Chad. He was trying to watch the luscious go-go dancer's hemline inch up to her crotch as she slowly climbed down from her bamboo perch — one of the bouncers, an Occidental with a shaved head, was helping her to the floor.

Two American soldiers — the only two, it seemed, who were not participating in the bar fight — stood behind Bullethead, arms folded across their chests as they licked their lips in anticipation. It was immediately obvious to both war dogs the two GIs had just arranged for a short-time in the rack, or perhaps even an all-nighter with the gorgeous dancer. "Must be nice," giggled Cory, as he rose up on two unsteady feet and swayed from side to side.

Chandler watched April follow the two paying customers up the stairwell that led to the quickie stalls on the second floor, then he turned to inspect the other two women in suspended cages. They too were round-eyes.

Quite a racket they got going here, he decided, as he moved across the floor to steady Cory's dazed and battered frame. The nightclub was packed — business was booming, helped along, no doubt, by the white women available for dancing partners or . . . whatever fantasies the boonyrat mind could conjure up.

He thought about the grunts he had recently left down in the delta, and though he knew they made do with their meager share of hamlet boom-boom girls, life outside Cho Gao could never compare with this. His eyes located a table of foreign correspondents, each with an American go-go dancer on his knee, and as he thought about Darnette, his anger boiled. *They* should have to spend a Tour-365 out in the field, he

197

decided, just like the GIs! The way they were laughing and carrying on, drinks in their hands and warm flesh in their lap—while teen-agers from Hometown U.S.A. fought and died only a dozen miles away—incensed him. But then again, that was the difference between warriors and civilians, and he had to keep reminding himself of that. A soldier was afforded the privilege of choosing his place, time and manner of death. What followed was imminent ascension into an elite plane of the spirit world where twilight was spent patrolling the jungles beyond the castlelike clouds. All the news media had to look forward to was the army of worms and maggots that awaited their corpses six feet under; a recent survey taken by members of their own press corps revealed an overwhelming majority of reporters did *not* believe in a supreme being or all-powerful life force, and therefore would never have to face the consequences for their false or biased journalistic projects while on earth. Always the elitists they felt they had no one to answer to, God or mortal.

MPs were rushing into the nightclub now, nightstick at the ready, but Big Chad was not impressed with their grand entrance—he had seen it all a hundred times before. Instead, he was watching the shapely woman making her way up the stairs. The higher she climbed, the farther up her miniskirt he could see.

Chandler rubbed at the aching between his temples: it was a sight for sore eyes.

But then her petite steps faltered somewhat, and he glanced up to check her expression. She was looking back over her shoulder at the swinging front doors to the bar. Her face was a shocked mask of both astonishment and recognition.

Chandler turned just in time to see Justin Ross enter the establishment moments after the military policemen. Behind him were Brent, Matt and Amy Atencio.

Big Chad started to raise his hand and his spirits in surprised greeting, but the sudden blast that ripped through the nightclub sent him backwards, off balance, and he slammed into Cory MacArthur. Both men tumbled over a table, onto the sticky floor.

Bleeding profusely from several shrapnel wounds, the last thing Chandler heard before he blacked out was Zemm's voice as she screamed his name in terror.

13

Several dozen emergency vehicles were throwing ghostly beams of crimson through the drifting smoke outside the nightclub when Chad Chandler opened his eyes. His head was throbbing with intense pain, but the tenement walls rising up all around him were a bouncing blur because they were carrying him out of the devastated structure on an ambulance stretcher. He tried to rise to a sitting position, but an unyielding hand clamped down on his shoulder, keeping him on his back. He knew it was the lieutenant.

"Zemm!" he yelled, and the word sent the pain in his head swirling about even faster—like the countless fire trucks still skidding up all around. "What about Zemm?"

"We haven't found her yet, Chad," Justin Ross whispered next to his ear. "She and Cory are still missing." His tone did not sound optimistic.

"But we'll find them, buddy!" Collins was beside his

other ear, patting his shoulder. "It's just a matter of time! Gotta wait for the smoke to clear, pal, that's all. We'll find 'em!"

"And we'll find 'em *alive*!" Amy was next to Brent. "Don't worry, Chad. Just let these dudes patch you up so we can get back to business."

"I thought Our Gang was all back in the Philippines, kicking ass," Chandler muttered as a bolt of pain lanced through his insides. He was covered with puncture wounds from the exploding satchel charge, but none of the shrapnel had damaged vital organs. "What are you guys doing in Saigontown, anyway? Shoulda known you'd slip in right at the wrong time and stir up the shit when me and the ol' lady were attemptin' to sip a little Saigon tea." He forced a chuckle, and the war dogs clustered around him laughed along. The two Vietnamese ambulance attendants also grinned, but they held apprehensive looks in their eyes. They could both sense the danger lurking around the group of soot-streaked Americans.

"After we extracted Amy's lovely ass from your classic case of unlawful detention down Manila way," Matt Sewell, the team's chopper pilot explained, "we flop-flopped it back to our little oasis in the middle of Khmerland, only to find you, Mac and the girls had booked a *baht* bus down here to the capital for a little R&R. So we decided to join you — Old Man Y back at the Pentagon still hasn't coded us a mission yet — though I must admit it took a while to track you down this week."

"Shoulda known the shit would hit the prop with Brent baby in the big picture." Chandler flipped the ex-policeman an obscene gesture as they loaded him into the back of the ambulance. "Goddamned coppers are always trailin' bad luck along wherever they go." He winced as the Vietnamese attendants strapped him in, and blood squirted forth from a string of puncture wounds along his right side.

"Aw, give Collins some credit." Sewell always spoke up when you least expected it. The others were already rushing back into the nightclub, despite a screen of oily, black smoke billowing forth from where two walls and half the roof had collapsed. "After the explosion, *he* was the one that dashed back outside and dusted the two cowboys on the Honda who flung the bomb through the swinging front doors. He coulda just ducked like the rest of us. Why hell, if it was me I woulda probably just—"

But Chandler interrupted him by reaching up and grabbing the chopper jockey's shirt front. He pulled Sewell closer, until they were nose to nose. The effort nearly drained him of what little energy he had left. "Find her, Matt!" The helpless sigh seemed to leave him from more holes than just his mouth, but Sewell knew it was only his imagination, despite the manner in which the ex-mercenary's chest was now soaked in blood. "Please find her for me." His strength wavered, and he laid back down, eyes shut tightly as he fought off the overpowering waves of pain. "She's the only thing beautiful to come out this ugly war," he groaned, moments before losing consciousness. "The only thing. . . . *person* that has made my life sentence with the war dogs bearable."

"You've got my word, Chad." Sewell clasped the big man's fist and they crossed index fingers in a manner normally reserved for American GIs and their Vietnamese *manois*. "We'll find her. If it takes the rest of the night, we'll find her. I promise! Just cut yourself some slack, brother. Let these dudes sew you up and fix you good as new with some legal 'ludes. Before you know it, we'll have her beside your hospital bed."

"This whole thing sucks, Matt." Chandler was falling backwards into the black pit. Sewell could sense it. "It's . . . just . . . not . . . fair, damnit."

"I know, Chad." He watched the fallen warrior slip loose from reality. "It's just not fair."

Sewell shut the doors to the ambulance and watched it pull away. Siren off, it slowly meandered in and out of the fire trucks, police landrovers and idling MP Assault tanks, then turned off down a dark, deserted back alley and accelerated, heading for Third Field Army Hospital.

Matt Sewell swallowed hard. He did not want to turn and walk back down to the smoldering nightclub and join in on the search. There were too many complications cropping up here. Too many downers. *Too many gut-wrenching emotions!* Life with the war dogs had always been cut and dried: quick in, terminate the target and quick out. But now Roscoe's splendid little group was getting to know each other. Friendships were being formed. Everyone was starting to *care*. To care about each other. A chilling shudder went through his limbs and down his spine, and he began to wonder if this new turn of events might mean the eventual downfall of the team.

Ross had never allowed them to get close before — as friends. Only mentally, so that the squad could continue to function like a well-oiled machine — a killing tool for the armchair warriors back at The Big P. But even Ross had been showing signs of affection recently, clues his wall of armor was slowly crumbling. Especially after their extended R&R in the Cambodian rain forest, and the unexpected hiatus spent with Princess Raina's people at the Khmer cliff palace.

The familiar flop-chopping whir of rotors overhead jarred Sewell from his thoughts, and he glanced up to see an Army Huey hovering above the scene. Dual spotlights attached to its skids flashed on, bathing the scene in brilliant silver, and as the powerful beams swished about, crisscrossing dramatically through the rising smoke and piles of rubble, Sewell spotted a charred limb rising up through a mound of debris. Sighing deeply, he shrugged his shoulders in resignation and started toward it.

They never found Zemm.

Seventy-two hours after the terrorist explosion, Saigon's police chief declared rescue operations at an end. Twenty dead had been found beneath the collapsed roof and walls. Three people were missing. The number was expected to grow once area AWOLs became official and the soldier's disappearance could be connected with the tragedy and not a desire to desert to the sleazy Saigon underworld.

Chad Chandler was released from Third Field Hospital the morning after the VC attacked the nightclub with their hit-and-run raid. Stiff and clumsy from bandages crisscrossing his torso from throat to belly, he fled his ward only after a heated argument with an Army doctor assigned to his case. Big Chad escaped down a casualty elevator moments before a radio jeep with two MPs in it arrived to quell the disturbance. He spent the next three days searching through the rubble for Zemm, and ignoring his comrade's every attempt at reasoning with him.

Ross never once interfered with the man. He knew returning to the scene of the massacre was the best medicine, regardless of how painful, both mentally and physically, it had to be.

With each dusk, when it became too dangerous to climb about the ruins, Amy would be waiting for him at the edge of the rubble, where police ropes kept the curious at bay. Lieutenant Ross had spoken with the precinct commander, and the *canh-sats* never once bothered the obsessed American. Salvage crews were scheduled to arrive the following week. The Army officer hoped Chad would work out his grief by then. He would just have to wait and see. Amy would lead him into the bar across the street, and they would drink rice wine until nothing seemed important anymore — even lost love and a wife he had yet to really learn to know and appreciate.

Collins and Sewell never joined the two. They were always busy on the edge of town, at the Agency pad outside Fort Hustler near Tan Son Nhut, repairing the Dragonfly. Their chopper had sustained thirty-some direct hits during the last escapade over Manila. It was a miracle they made it back to the Nam unscathed. Ross had ordered them to get the craft back in top shape. Mr. Y's next mission would be arriving anyday now, and he wanted to be ready, regardless of all the personal problems the team was suffering. And enduring.

The lieutenant himself remained out of the limelight, though he was always at a corner table, watching Amy and Chad. He could tell a lot from the look in a man's eyes, and he was extremely worried about the team's combat engineer. Could Chandler function under stress so soon after losing his wife? Ross would have to make a decision soon: keep the ex-merc active in his prime role as demo man, or sideline him for the next game. And in this contest, there was no bench.

Ross would have to take Chandler out of the picture. Permanently.

And then there was the child.

Christ, as if he didn't have enough problems! Ross gnawed on a knuckle as he watched Amy order another round of Singapore slings and playfully reach across the table and twist her drinking partner's ear. Chandler's tight smile faded abruptly each time she did—usually once a night—and Ross found the reaction bewildering. *Just another mental quirk?*

The baby was with Cory's woman. She was now safely back at a new hotel room, on the other side of town. They had found MacArthur with his legs protruding from a pile of heavy cinder blocks. When they dug him out, it was learned he had sustained only a simple fracture of his right arm. A cast was required, but he would probably not miss the next mission, as the break was midway between the wrist and elbow and did not prohibit dexterity in the field. Sewell had already painted it camouflage shades of green and brown.

His Cambodian girlfriend related over and over what she had witnessed directly after the bomb blast. Zemm had scurried up the stairwell leading to the second floor behind several American dancers moments before the nearest walls and roof collapsed. She could not be sure if Zemm had been hit by all the falling debris or not.

But things did not look good. The Vietnamese national police told Ross most of the second floor was now in the nightclub's wine cellar. The bodies of three white women had been found beneath the bricks and corrugated tin. A mountainous ton of rubble still remained to be cleared by salvage crews. If their friend's body was beneath it, there was little hope she was still alive.

"I never should have been in that lousy dive," Chandler told Amy over and over again. "Out of boredom, waiting for you guys to come back from Manila, I took a hop down to the delta at the invitation of a reporter-type who survived a bandit ambush with us on the bus ride down from Cambodia," he related to her. "When I got back, I felt like a night time visit to the closest watering hole would really hit the spot. Zemm protested, but I dragged her along, and the next thing I know my world's crumbling all around me under a rain of hot metal.

"She didn't deserve that, Amy." Tears welled up in his eyes again, like they did every night. "She didn't deserve to die that way."

Amy said nothing, but a glimmer of hope caused her eyes to sparkle and she shook off the effects of the alcohol without being obvious. He was finally accepting the probability Zemm was dead. He was finally coming to terms with the horror of it all.

"It's all that fuckin' reporter's fault!" he exploded without warning, tightening his fingers around his glass until it splintered and blood trickled out between

207

them. "I'll *kill* the sonofabitch!" he roared, standing up, and patrons at the tables surrounding them turned to look their way.

Amy reached across the tablecloth and patted his cut hand in an attempt to calm him. "Reporter?" she asked softly, hoping the unexcited word would have an effect on the big soldier, but the ploy didn't work. Chandler rose to his feet.

"Shoulda been *him* that died!" Chandler yelled as he started for the counter. "Shoulda been him!"

He pushed a top-heavy bargirl out of the way, and as she stumbled back and slid across the floor on her haunches, dropping a platter loaded down with empty glasses, an American Marine rose to challenge him. "Hey, asshole!" The lance corporal grabbed his shoulder from behind. "That's no way to treat a lady!"

Chandler swung around violently, and his fist connected with the soldier's cheek. He flew backwards over a table, unconscious from the hammerlike assault, long before he crashed across the floor.

Chandler confronted four civilians in safari "TV suits" who were seated at the far end of the counter, attempting to mind their own business. That a slender female had just lost face and split her hot pants down the middle was none of their concern. They were pacifists by habit. They only wrote about action and conflict — they rarely participated in it: the networks and wire services did not pay enough. Ten times as much as the Armed Forces, granted, but still not enough.

"Where's that snake-belly Darnette?" Chandler screamed. One of the foreign correspondents took to trembling visibly, and spilled his drink.

208

"Who?" the reporter beside him asked, feigning total ignorance.

"You heard me, scumbag. *Darnette!* I wanna know where he's at. *Where does he hang out?*" Chandler rushed over beside the man who had spilled his glass and yelled into his ear, "Tell me, *now!* Or your final night in the Pearl of the Orient has suddenly arrived!"

"He's at the Continental!" the man cried out as Chandler got him in a choke hold with one massive arm around his throat.

"Where?" Big Chad had heard him the first time, but wanted to make sure there was no doubt in his mind.

"The Continental!" the man repeated when challenged. "On the roof top terrace. He's always there, drinkin' with the Aussies. *On the Continental!*"

"But he's out in the field this week!" the reporter next to Chandler's captive exploded, jumping from his seat and scurrying out of reach to safety.

"What?" Big Chad released the headlock, and the small man dropped to the floor with a loud thump.

"I heard his bureau chief talking about it last night. Something about intercepting a Lurp patrol down around . . . . Vung Tau. That's right, the beach. *Vung Tau!*"

Chandler raced from the room and Amy started after him, but paused in the doorway when she spotted Justin Ross sitting alone at a corner table. He answered her questioning look with a bemused, resigned nod, and she charged out into the night, trying to keep up with Big Chad.

Ross sighed while listening to the Wild-West-type swinging doors squeaking back and forth after their hasty departure, and he brought his glass up to his lips and sipped slowly, casually, though the thoughts were crashing about in his mind like a high speed chase. *Vung Tau.*

He could see the white sand beach even now.

The same vast, immaculate stretch of peacefulness where his people had so suddenly met violent death nearly two years ago. Before the Diem hit. Before he had come back from the near-fatal bullet wounds to put together another team of war dogs.

Vung Tau. He would never forget her.

The swinging entrance doors gave way to the sound of soft music, and he looked up to see three American women stepping onto the stage in front of the dozen or so tables crowding the bar.

The woman on the left was black, with a more than ample chest straining to bust loose from her tank top with each gyration to the beat of drums now coming from the huge wall speakers. Ross could tell from her mannerisms that she was an American.

The woman on the right appeared to be Latino, but she in no way reminded him of Amy Atencio. Her body was as firmly developed, especially the chest — if not more so — but there was a dark, uncaring silliness in her expression Amy was not capable of. Like she was telling every admirer below the stage that she was available — for the right price. And Amy no longer operated that way. Ross watched her shapely thighs and tight hips swirl about below the miniskirt, and he decided then and there he had never seen such an oversexed dancer in his rather limited career as a bar hopper. Tonight just might be the night he'd treat himself to a little *real* Rest & Relaxation.

But then the woman in the middle caught his attention. So young, he decided. Such a waste. Definitely no cherry girl—he could sense it in the way she moved with the music—and the tracks along one arm were clearly visible even at this distance, but the face . . . There was something about the face that made him want to take her away from here. Pull her down from that stage, fight off the bouncers who would surely appear and whisk her away to a safe house somewhere, where he could nurse her back to health. Protect her.

Not that she really needed him. Ross's eyes dropped from her well-endowed chest to the flaring thighs that made the hot pants so tight. She would command a high price in any bordello in the Orient. He wondered what brought her to a city like Saigon. Unless it was the lure of fast bucks. *Always the money.* He wondered if she was preferential with her customers, or if her pimp even allowed discretion. Or if she even had a pimp. Maybe she *was* just another burnt-out singer-turned-dancer after all. Maybe Asia was just where she ended up after years of competing on the vicious entertainers circuit. So many possibilities, such a complex drama.

A Vietnamese hostess glided by, tall, brown bottles of *ba muoi ba* filling a lacquerwood platter that was balanced precariously on the top of her head.

Now, that's what femininity is all about, really, he decided as he watched her narrow haunches moving back and forth within the tight, wraparound throat-to-ankle *ao dai.* The traditional gowns, gossamer thin, but worn over black silky, form-hugging pantaloons drove him crazy. They revealed little, if any, flesh, yet they drove him wilder than any dozen go-go dancers gyrating in their floor-show cages could. Maybe he'd ask her what she was doing after work, but then he spotted the intricately carved wedding band of 22K Vietnamese gold, and the seven traditional bracelets that told him she was not looking for an American, and the Army lieutenant fell back into his fit of depression.

He glanced at his watch, finished off the beer on the table in front of him, then got to his feet and started for the door. It was time to taxi out to Tan Son Nhut and check on Sewell and Collins. Had to always keep after the daring duo, or they'd sell The Fly on the Saigon black market for gambling money.

Ross was feeling a slight buzz from the liquor, but he was in total control of his faculties. He sensed a fight brewing in the middle of the dance floor between two Marines and a Special Forces sergeant, so he detoured around them, coming right alongside the stage.

A scream sliced through the loud din of musical notes filling the bar, and Ross glanced up to see the dancer in the middle was now frozen to the spot, hands covering her mouth in shock.

And she was staring straight down at Justin Ross.

"Father!" The word came out in a scream again, and this time Ross slid to a stop on the beer-smeared tile.

April Adams rushed forward a few feet, then hesitated before throwing her arms out at him, and then Ross saw it. In the lines around her eyes—the way the cheeks curved when she smiled, though she was not really smiling now. She was sobbing in relief. But he saw it. The facial contours that hadn't really changed with age, with the years. There was none of the sparkle in the depths of her eyes he thought he would

212

see if ever they met again, but there was no mistaking her. This was his baby!

His daughter! Grown now, and blooming into a woman, but she was still the child he remembered—the little girl he hadn't seen in twelve years!

Ross reached up and embraced her, fighting off the tears welling up in his eyes and the uncertainty and shock clouding his thinking as he lifted her down from the stage onto the dance floor. April tightened her arms around his neck as she held on, never wanting to let go again, and Justin closed his eyes just as rigidly, forcing his mental picture of her out: the revealing costume she wore, the curves of her flesh, the syringe tracks on her arms.

But then Ross felt danger moving in on his left, and he whirled around seconds before the tall man with the shaved head reached him.

"What the hell you think you're doing, pal?" Cotton clamped a powerful hand on Ross's shoulder, but the lieutenant lashed out with a swift side kick that connected with the hood's groin and sent him crashing to the floor, groaning.

"I'm not sure you're who I think you are," Ross smiled at April as he led her toward the front exit; he was having his doubts now. "I just don't see how it could be."

"It's me, Father!" she cried without breaking down entirely. "I knew I would find you. I knew you *existed*! I've been searching for you all these years!"

"Well, we have to talk, honey." He wrapped an arm around her as they stepped out into the night. Ross flagged down a taxi as several *kamikaze* cyclo drivers rushed across the street toward him. "Somewhere

213

where it's quiet. Somewhere where we can catch up on time.

"You don't want to go out there!" The Special Forces sergeant held onto his bush hat as another sheet of monsoon rain lashed across their position.

"Why not?" Chandler buttoned up one of the flak vests an enlisted man had handed him and squinted at the circle of distant smoke. "Why the fuck not?"

The NCO glanced down at the slender woman squatting beside Chandler and shrugged, " 'Cause Charlie's thick as canal leeches out there, sir!" All three of them pressed closer to the ground as another wave of shrapnel passed inches over their heads and secondary mortar blasts mingled with the rolling thunder. "You *don't* wanna go out there, sir! I guarantee it!"

"You say that's where the reporter Darnette is holed up with a squad of your people?" Chandler yelled above the whistle of crisscrossing projectiles.

"Well, yes, sir. But you don't wanna go out beyond the wire, sir! We can't ensure your safety once you're out past the perimeter! Best you wait till this storm clears out. Yeah, best you wait!"

Chandler glanced back over a shoulder and watched the helicopter that had dropped them and several hundred pounds' worth of supplies off at the Green Beret outpost ascend directly into the storm front. Gone was their ticket out—until the next supply or Dustoff slick. "You with me?" He locked eyes with Amy, and then, having second thoughts, said, "You better stay here."

"I promised that goofy Roscoe I'd keep your fat ass

out of trouble, Chad. You *know* I'm true to my word!" She slammed a magazine into the carbine the sergeant handed her.

"If you'd just be patient, we'll have some gunships up here *rikky-tik*!" the sergeant pleaded without actually getting emotional. He really didn't care what they did one way or the other, and both war dogs detected it in his tone.

"Darnette might not still be breathing by then!" Chandler yelled back. "And the two of us got important business to discuss!"

Amy glanced from Chad's eyes to those of the Green Beret, hoping to find some difference in them — something signalling the cutting edge between sanity and madness. But all she saw was the adrenaline rush of imminent battle, impending doom. She saw the same thing in the angry skies closing in on them, felt it in the hot, sticky air: they were all going to die here.

"At least wait until dusk!" the sergeant urged as another set of mortar rounds impacted with dull thumps on either side of their hilltop position. "Maybe then the odds will shift slightly to your side. You haven't got that much time to lose: it's already seventeen hundred hours!"

Chandler thought it over for a second, absorbed Amy's agreeing nod, then let out a hearty sigh and unwound, allowing the stress and hate to flow out from him in all directions. They would wait. It wouldn't do to come this far only to stop a lucky sniper's round with his skull. With this storm rolling through, darkness would fall even faster than usual.

The supply chopper had brought Chandler and Atencio in during the height of a battle between the camp defenders and a battalion of hard-core NVA who had infiltrated the coastal area south and east of Saigon, and had surprised a Green Beret jungle patrol as it returned from H&I raids against the local Viet Cong. Darnette had gone out with the Special Forces team on their midnight missions for several nights running now. He was also with them when they were ambushed only a few hundred yards down the valley from their base camp by the North Vietnamese regulars.

With the rain still heavy and flares fighting to stay aloft on the edge of the storm, Chandler, Amy and two Green Berets—both medics—set out under cover of darkness to reach the pinned-down Americans. Because of the high winds and pounding rainfall, the gunships did not arrive as scheduled. The men were encouraged to hold on until dawn—the hill would no longer be socked in, according to the satellite pros back at Disneyland East's weather center. Another rescue attempt would be mounted then. Ground troops were already en route from Xuyen Moc.

It was slow going. From the hilltop, the NVA could be seen cautiously encircling the besieged Americans just prior to dark. If they did not mount an all-out offensive to overrun the defenders before help could arrive with the sunrise, they'd surely booby-trap the trails leading down to the men so as many casualties as possible could be brought down without so much as a shot being fired. Radio communications with the highly-trained soldiers had been lost moments before the first series of thunderbolts shot down into the valley.

Chad Chandler low-crawled at a pace much faster

than was prudent. He knew this, of course, but he didn't care. His all-consuming passion was to confront Darnette. He tried not to think about the possibility the man was already dead. And he did not worry about Amy—he knew from past experience she was more than capable of holding her own.

As he grew nearer the two groups of guerrillas, Chandler watched scattered bursts of outgoing green tracers mark the positions of the communists. Now and then a lone red tracer would fly back—telling him there were indeed survivors down there. One round even ricocheted up the hill toward him, bounced off a rock only ten feet away and arced out into the night before it disappeared over a hill.

When he was close enough to hear the communists making careless metallic scraping noises—they were becoming overconfident and apparently preparing a nighttime snack of rice packed in rolled banana leaves—Chandler leaped to his feet and charged down the hillside, firing a carbine in each hand on full automatic. Bright white tracers exploded forth at the startled Asians as they were attacked from behind, and some of the rounds exploded against the cooking pots with bright showers of sparks, adding to the terror and confusion.

Chandler screamed war cries as he charged down through the enemy—obscenities in Vietnamese that were so frightening many of the teen-agers scattered rather than fight back at this rain forest ghost.

When he ran out of ammo, Chandler swung his rifle back and forth as he raced down through the valley trail, ignoring the threat of trip wires. Jaws and arm bones cracked left and right in the pitch-black darkness, and Big Chad's war cries even sent a chill down the spines of the dug-in Americans he was rapidly approaching.

A strand of barbed wire caught his lower leg, gouging into the flesh, and he tumbled over the top of a mound of sandbags as a flare shot skyward, illuminating the killing zone.

"Friendly forces!" one of the besieged soldiers yelled at the top of his lungs as Amy and the two medics flew in behind Chandler. "Hold your fire!"

"Christ! I never seen anything like that!" A buck sergeant with his face charcoaled black flashed Big Chad a toothy grin. "D'you play for the Rams, boy?" and then he spotted the firm, flapping protrusions on Amy's chest as she rolled out of the line of fire for cover. "What's this? I mean, *what are these?*"

"A female!" a fellow noncom replied as Atencio hugged the ground. He nodded upon recognizing the two medics and pointed behind the main foxhole to a charred and blackened bunker the returning patrol had taken refuge in. "Back there, buddy. Half a dozen WIAs for you! Our medic took one of the first rounds, damn these dinks!"

But all attention was quickly focusing on Amy. "Who *are* you guys, uh, persons?" They seemed to find the black coveralls as intriguing as the jutting breasts.

"Where's Darnette?" Chandler yelled, rage in his eyes. But his expression didn't seem to faze any of the Special Forces men.

"The reporter?" a sergeant replied dryly, unamused with the direction their conversation was taking.

"Yeah!" Big Chad slammed a fresh magazine of bullets into his smoking carbine.

"Back there with the casualties, pal."

"He's dead?" Chandler's jaw dropped, and he turned to rush away.

"Naw, but that's where the deepest hole is!" Several of the men laughed at the insult, but then their position was inundated with crisscrossing tracers, and everyone hugged the earth, forcing dirt up their noses.

Except Chandler. He continued back toward the bunker, walking upright. Tracers ricocheted about his boots and one even bounced between his legs, but none struck him.

Chad dropped down into the dark bunker. He immediately spotted Darnette cowering in the far corner, his camera gear shielding his head from falling shrapnel.

"Darnette!" Chandler yelled, bolting a live round into his weapon's chamber loudly.

"Yeah! That's me!" The reporter did not bother to look up as another trio of mortars crashed in beside the bunker and a sheet of rain pounded down after it.

"You're a son of a bitch, mister!" Chandler accused the man, and he remained on his feet, ignoring the flying lead, as he spoke.

"Wha—?" Darnette glanced up for the first time, his face incredulous at the words being directed at him.

"You're nothing but a snake-bellied *bastard*!" A stray round slammed into Chandler's shoulder, knocking him backwards slightly, but he remained on his feet. He brought his carbine to his shoulder and aimed it at Darnette.

"Hey!" One of the Green Beret sergeants rushed up and knocked the rifle skyward right as it discharged. "What the hell's going on here?"

219

"The asshole's a motherfucking communist!" Chandler pointed a finger down at the reporter as Darnette scampered on his knees for cover. "Nothing but a motherfucking communist! You oughta throw him to the Cong out there!" Smoke floated in front of the new hole in his flak jacket.

"We're fightin' the NVA tonight, mister!"

"Whatever!" Chandler was not one to be bothered about specifics. "I came all the way out here to—"

A deafening wall of sound rose up all around the Americans, cutting Chandler off, and they automatically placed their backs to each other so they could face out at the night.

"What the fu—" one of the Green Berets started to mutter, though he had heard the inhuman crescendo before.

"I was just doing my job!" Darnette chose that moment to speak. "I just write what I see. The camera don't never blink, my friend!"

"Shut up!" Chandler roared as the ghostly wail increased on all sides. "Shut up and pray you see tomorrow, coward!"

Bugles began trumpeting out of tune all around, and the shriek that was a thousand enemy voices building up their death chant exploded on the other side of the wire.

"They're attacking!" the Green Beret sergeant yelled, suddenly ignoring the newcomers as he rushed back to his own men. "The zips are makin' their move! Prepare to repel!"

The ground began to shake as the battalion of communist soldiers rushed down the hillsides toward the Americans. Chandler threw one of his carbines to

Darnette, and the heavy stock bounced off the reporter's left arm. Darnette cried out in pain, but Chandler felt no compassion for the man. "Use it!" he ordered. "For the first time in your no-account life, chuck the magic box and make yourself useful!"

A skinny form flew through the air from the dark at the edge of the bunker and a tire-tread sandal connected with the side of Chandler's head, but the stocky American merely sidestepped the brunt of the blow, butt-stroking the Vietnamese in the face as he flew past.

A spray of tracers fanned inches above the heads of the defenders as they rushed about in a crouch. And Amy jumped up and returned fire in scattered three- and four-round bursts.

"Will ya look at them titties bounce!" one Green Beret muttered to another with guarded admiration.

"To hell with the flappin' flesh, Jimmy! Check out the dame's trigger-finger talent!"

One of the medics popped a hand flare without warning, and as the blinding projectile shot skyward, a hundred hostile faces were illuminated less than a dozen feet away, charging the flimsy strand of concertina with fixed bayonets.

14

Amy knew it was the end.

Her mouth went dry and her legs began to go numb, but she concentrated on firing the carbine shot by single shot and not on the more popular automatic mode. In the back of her head, she felt her final thoughts before death should be of Brent, the last man she loved, but instead, she was seeing herself taken captive by the enemy soldiers. Amy was not stupid. She knew they would take their time with her — probing her rich body for the secrets it held before executing her. They would slaughter the men around her immediately. But they would save *her* for dessert.

She shot an eye out of one Asian, then whirled to the left and killed another before her firing pin slammed home on an empty chamber.

"Goodbye, guys!" she muttered in resignation, throwing her weapon at the nearest Vietnamese. "It's been fun — *though we hardly knew ya!*"

She had just about accepted the fact they were outnumbered and cold meat when dual flashes of blinding light erupted on the edge of the bunker and two deafening explosions set her ears to ringing.

"Claymores!" A Green Beret was laughing almost demonically behind her as the thousands of tiny steel balls sliced through the enemy soldiers, catapulting them backwards off their feet. "Surprise, *motherfuckers!*"

But another wave of communists appeared to replace their fallen comrades almost instantly.

Chandler fired off several three-round bursts, knocking over a score of NVA infantrymen before he yelled back at Darnette, "I don't hear you smokin' no one back there, Mr. Huntley-Brinkley!"

Darnette made no reply, and when Chandler turned to look down at him, the reporter was pointing his rifle directly at Big Chad's face.

"Always knew you were nothin' but a no-good commie trash bag," Chandler muttered, painfully aware there was no time to react. A split second later, Darnette pulled the trigger.

Amy turned just in time to see the high-caliber tracer splash against Chandler's forehead and explode in a shower of green sparks out the back of his skull. Still grinning, the ex-mercenary's stocky frame flopped down onto its back, gun hand twitching. Three circles of gray smoke floated up from the gaping entrance wound and quickly broke apart on the night breeze.

"Chad!" Amy screamed, rushing forward, her eyes on Darnette—her fingernails extended, bristling for the attack.

A searing blast of heat streaked past her right ear from behind, and Amy was horrified to see the shoulder-launched RPG slam into Darnette's chest.

223

His body was thrown backwards against the bunker's sandbags, and an instant later the jarring explosion threw his severed limbs out at the other Americans.

"My God!" Amy shuddered as the bloody spray covered the hands across her eyes and face. "I don't *believe* this! I don't fucking *believe* . . ." Rivulets of blood were trickling down her legs from small puncture wounds on the front of her thighs, but she was feeling no pain yet. The adrenaline rush was preventing that.

She glanced around behind her: the two S.F. medics who had accompanied her and Chandler down from the base camp were both dead from multiple gunshot wounds. Only one buck sergeant and a communications corporal remained standing, and the NCO had sustained a serious throat wound.

"Hey hey hey! Screw the damn NVA!"

Amy was amazed the sergeant could still joke about the situation as he stumbled to the other side of the bunker, searching for the triggering device of the remaining claymore anti-personnel mines, but she had heard some truly unbelievable war stories about these legendary heroes, so perhaps his behavior wasn't that unusual after all. But his bravery shocked her; the man continued to rush from abandoned post to post, ignoring the blood that spurted weakly from his throat wound with each racing heartbeat.

Three successive blasts shook the ground beneath the Americans, and the night came alive with more injured Vietnamese screaming.

A burst of green tracers responded to the thundering concussions, and Amy stood by, horrified and helpless, as a rifle slug tore the corporal's lower jaw

224

away. She jumped forward and reached down to pick up his weapon as a second bullet split his Adam's apple in half, nearly decapitating the man.

"That leaves just you and me, baby!" the sergeant sang the words to her before turning to send several M-79 grenades flying from a sawed-off thumper out into the night. "Too bad we couldn't get to know each other a little better, prior to our rather sudden and unscheduled demise."

"Prior to our demise *hell*!" Amy snapped back as she crawled about the floor of the bunker, retrieving weapons. "I'm not quite ready to check out yet, buster!" She fired a few shots over the ridge of sandbags, then commenced stripping the dead men at her feet of grenades and bayonets. "And if I gotta go, I'm takin' out as many of the lousy commies as I can!"

She was amazed at her own tone of voice, and how much she suddenly sounded like Chad Chandler. Her cheek began to itch as she cautiously watched the dark blanket cloaking the bunker's perimeter. She knew it was tears.

Impressed with the power of the claymores, the North Vietnamese retreated into the treeline midway up the hillside, and the two Americans were able to hold out for the next several hours.

Until pre-dawn.

As an orange-pink glow began to light up the eastern horizon, Amy sensed the NVA starting down through the tamarinds again. The communists had been taunting them all through the night with obscenities, insults and random stick grenades, but they knew dawn meant reinforcements and, with the storm moving on, Cobra gunships.

A shrill whistle broke the eerie silence, and mortar after mortar began raining down all around the make-shift camp, but none of the projectiles struck the bunker.

And as if in rebuttal, a second downpour, moving in from the opposite direction, swept through the steep valley, socking the area in again with mist, a fine layer of ghostly gunsmoke and pounding sheets of marauding rain.

Amy had wrapped a bandolier of M26 grenades around her waist. The frags were her insurance. Against violation. Even now she could see the bobbing pith helmets with their little red stars starting down the hillsides through the dense rows of high trees. If she were a man, they wouldn't risk injury taking her alive, but being a woman — and a young, attractive, well-endowed round-eye at that — she knew the NVA, an army with as many morale weaknesses as any other, would go out of their way to capture her unharmed. And she was determined to die first, her new-found honor intact.

"What the —" the Green Beret's eyes glanced up at the sky as a black, metallic craft dropped down from the blanket of clouds, gyrocoasting in a tight, gliding circle down to the ground. "What the —"

"Roscoe!" Amy screamed, elated, as she recognized the team's Dragonfly swooping up through the mist parting for the rotor's power downblast. "Roscoe, *you crazy sonofabitch!*"

Its turbines kicked in, and the Huey's nose cannon began firing a non-stop flurry of high-explosive rounds as its tail swung in a continuous circle over the besieged bunker.

"Awright, *Roscoe!*" Amy raised a fist in salute when she recognized the lieutenant's grim features leaning out the open hatch, gauging the enemy troop movements — their strong points, their weaknesses. He was holding one of the new M-16s and spraying banana clip after banana clip down at the North Vietnamese on full automatic.

"Rock 'n' roll!" The sergeant smiled up at the hovering chopper as he waved his own fist at the retreating communists.

A rope ladder dropped down from the belly of The Fly and bounced off the top of his head. "*Choi oi!*" he yelled, ecstatic as rainwater pelted his face, making it glisten. "The chance of a lifetime!"

"My ninth!" Amy laughed away the tears as she scurried up the ladder. Overhead, Brent Collins and Cory MacArthur showered the ground with M60 fire from opposite hatch openings.

"Let's go! Let's go! Let's go!" Collins yelled down at the Green Beret sergeant as he grabbed hold of the bottom rung. When it looked as though the soldier got a good grip, he gave Sewell the thumbs-up, and the chopper pilot poured power into the craft's turbines. The rotors roared, lifting the helicopter up away from the bunker as tracers from the ground climbed the skyline toward them.

"Nine KIAs down there!" the SF sergeant pulled a handful of dog tags from his pocket and laid them at Ross's feet. "One MIA," he added, "but nine KIAs, confirmed, General. All bona fide heroes!"

"You did fine, Sergeant." Ross patted the man on the shoulder as he winked across the cabin at Amy. "You did positively outrageously fucking fine."

Sewell, genuinely inspired for one of the few times in his life, glanced over his shoulder at the wounded sergeant again before repeating a set of coordinates into his helmet's radio mike.

Five minutes later, a squadron of Phantom jets swooped in on the valley, unleashing ton upon ton of billowing napalm that lit up the pre-dawn brighter than a false sunrise.

Justin Ross rushed down the narrow, dimly lit corridor, the sound of his boots falling loudly against the teakwood competing with the throbbing between his temples.

When he came to the room at the end of the hallway, his foot came up and the flimsy door crashed inward in a shower of splinters.

Bullethead Cotton was sitting in a huge beanbag pillow against the far wall, his head leaned back between two stereo speakers that were putting out Aussie rock. The lieutenant held a sawed-off shotgun beside his hip. Cotton was unarmed and naked. A black woman was kneeling in front of him, her ebony haunches exposed to Ross as she sucked frantically on the pimp's bulging erection.

"What's the meaning of this?" Cotton asked calmly as the last of the shattered door fluttered to the ground. The woman, despite her drugged stupor, tried to glance back at the intruder, but Cotton's hands shot forward, clamping against the sides of her head. He continued working her mouth up and down as he stared at Ross, smiling, and with his facial expression barely changing, he ejaculated until the woman ran out of air and began to gag. "Swallow it, you stupid cunt!" He rammed her face down into his lap until he was through with her, then roughly cast her aside.

The woman tumbled onto her belly, rolled over with a groan and curled up into the fetal position, knees drawn up to her sagging breasts. Her skirt was lying next to his leg, and Cotton draped it over his crotch. "I asked you a question, mister." He remained as calm as before. "Who the flying fuck are you?"

"I don't believe you're in the position to be asking the questions around here, clit-breath." Ross moved a couple steps closer, the barrel of the shotgun rising to emphasize his point.

"Are we gonna play Simon Says, or what?" Cotton's tone rose angrily as if he hadn't even seen the double barrels stop a foot in front of his face. "Who the hell are you, bozo?"

"Your executioner."

The lieutenant pulled a revolver from his belt and dropped it on the floor between Cotton's ankles. The pimp flinched at the harsh noise of metal against wood.

"Does the name April Adams ring a bell, scrotum-lips?" Ross thought back to all the years his daughter had been without a father. After the incident in 1953 where he killed the unarmed Korean woman in a dark, enemy-controlled tunnel—a mistake that cost him a life sentence with the war dogs—the government had advised his wife he was Missing in Action and presumed dead. Beyond a reasonable doubt. And Ross had never made any attempt to re-contact her or visit his daughter. Something about it being best for them both, his mental block told him. He *knew* running things this way was for the best, though sometimes he wondered if it wasn't the coward's way out. His wife had moved away four years later and remarried, but April never gave up hope she would someday find the man who had stood behind her when she played in the yard with the small poodle, who bounced her on his knee in the park and who read her a different bedtime story every night . . ., who always fled from the Chinese soldiers only to get shot in the back, in her nightmares.

"April Adams?" Cotton laughed loudly. "She was one of my best whores, *papa-san*." An evil gleam of recognition shot across his eyes as he made the connection — finally realized the reason for the anger boiling over in Ross, why the stranger was taking it all so personally. "I taught her well, big boy." Cotton's satisfied grin grew ear to ear. "She gave the best blowjobs in Saigon. Would you like me to line you up with her? Is that what this is all about?"

Ross kicked the revolver and it slid across the floor and slammed against the pimp's testicles. Cotton's face flushed red but he kept his smile intact. "Pick it up," Ross said coldly.

"No way, Jose," Cotton laughed back, a Do-I-look-that-stupid? expression on his face now.

"Suit yourself, gutter slime."

The shotgun exploded, and Cotton's head bounced

off the wall with the thunderous discharge and rolled out of sight, under the bed, still grinning stupidly though all that remained above the lips was a bloody, gaping crater.

He found Zemm in one of the back rooms. Handcuffed to a bar that ran along one entire wall. Twelve other Vietnamese women were with her, waiting to be initiated into Cotton's sordid underworld pleasure palace. Across the room, those Americans that had not fled still sat in small, cramped, individual cells, waiting—dreading—their turn to be led to the quickie stalls down the hall, directly over the dance floor.

Using a set of keys he found in an adjacent office, Ross set them all free. He led Zemm over to a window overlooking Tu Do Street, where they could be alone.

He avoided her eyes and hopeful gaze as he stared down at the women with their brightly colored umbrellas crowding the rain-cleansed sidewalks below.

"My husband is dead." She sensed the announcement and made it herself calmly instead.

"Yes," Ross admitted. His head dropped slightly between his shoulders and he grasped the windowsill for support. "I'm sorry, Zemm."

They stood there in silence for several minutes, listening to the rain falling across the roof overhead, and she placed her small, fragile hands across his. "I am, too."

Then she walked away, and as he turned and left the room, Ross heard her break down and sob, totally alone, mourning the loss of her man.

They confronted him in the hallway outside. Collins and MacArthur. Sewell. The rose among the thorns: Amy. He did not even realize he raised himself slightly on his toes, gazing over their shoulders, searching for Big Chad.

"Sorry we're late," Cory's words came across as a whisper. "But you drive like a fucking maniac, Justin. It was hard keeping up."

"We heard the shot from downstairs." When Sewell cleared his throat, everyone in the hallway heard it.

"Are we too late?" Collins clasped Amy's hand without realizing it.

"It's over." Ross's eyes fell to the ground, and he held out a briefcase. "It's over as soon as I get these records over to CID, that is," he added.

"What are they?" Cory stepped closer, but Ross did not hand over the contents.

"Enough evidence that'll put two hairballs back stateside named Falconi and Glover away for a long, long time, my young friend."

Amy found a sudden, gnawing need to change the subject. "Anything from Old Man Y, Justin?" she asked. "Anything about the mission we been waiting all these weeks for? I think we need a little change of scenery, if you know what I mean."

"I need a little change of scenery, myself, Miss Atencio." He reached into a vest pocket. "I've some business to attend to." He pulled out a five-by-seven manila envelope stuffed to overflowing. "Here's the lowdown on our next target. Study the photos and the bio, I'll get back to you in a couple nights. That hit's set for next week."

232

"This is the big one, eh, Justin?" Cory grabbed the envelope. "This is the one we been waitin' for all this time?"

"This is the one, kid. Enjoy."

"What's the target's name?" Sewell asked as Ross rounded the corner in the hallway and started down the stairs.

"Darnette!" Ross called back. "Some dirtbag reporter they discovered is a high-ranking KGB plant. Been writing some godawful propaganda 'bout our boys in the boonies. He's down in Mytho, or Vung Tau. It's our assignment to track his ass down and cancel his ticket. Make it look like the VC did it. Or better yet, the North Vietnamese."

There followed an unnatural silence, then, halfway down the stairs, Ross heard Amy burst into sudden laughter. Like they had just whispered a private little joke to each other behind his back, or a guarded secret had just been revealed. His rush to the ground floor did not flow. He did not want to know.

The windshield wipers swishing back and forth had almost put him to sleep when the taxi slid abruptly to the side of the road.

"Majestic Hotel, mista!" the cabbie sounded much too cheerful in contrast to the depressing weather. "Numba One Tu Do!"

The intensity that was Saigon flooded through him as Ross mounted the steps to the hotel lobby. Shoeshine boys scurried about his legs, pawing at his pants for handouts of *dong* coins or bubblegum; prostitutes

233

with their legs jacked provocatively on street corner curbs displayed just the right amount of smooth, amber-toned thigh to prospective customers. *You buy me Saigon tea, Joe?* Black-market hawkers loitered at the entrances to alleyways, peddling their stolen goods, dope and kiddie porn. The streets were clogged with sputtering motor scooters, and roadblocks at every other intersection bristled with parked tank cannons and armed militiamen. Gunships hovered above it all, ever watchful, eagerly waiting for the midnight curfew when all the streets of the concrete jungle became just another freefire zone. And jet fighters raced their engines at Tan Son Nhut, hoping to miss that random, solitary rocket the wily VC shot into the heart of the city once a week, preferably at three in the morning, when you were snuggled up beside your *Vo chura cuoi* — or better yet, on top of her, pumping away, unprepared for the uninvited, ultimate orgasm.

It was not the kind of town you'd normally want to raise your child in. A hundred thousand war-orphans-turned-prostitutes were testimony enough to that.

And April was already a young lady. But they could escape to another place, another time, and pretend at starting all over. Until he was called back to the war dogs again. Until fate tore him away from her again. He thought about how Chad always talked about just quitting the team so he could retreat deep into the Cambodian rain forest with his woman to lead a peaceful family life. Ross chuckled inside: that was Chandler's honest-to-God version of a normal existence. But it just wouldn't work for the lieutenant.

Justin Ross took the steps to the third floor two at a

time now as he thought about the fancy dinner in the open-air restaurant across the street and evening at the fancy Rex cinema that awaited them. He was finally going to be able to prove to April — and himself — what a good father he could really be. Even after all these years.

His fingers were actually shaking as he fumbled with the keys to the room he had gotten her miles away from Cotton's whorehouse.

It never occurred to him to knock first, and when he finally got the door open, he could see the curve and swell of her buttocks as she lay sleeping on her stomach across the bed, naked.

Blushing for the first time in decades, he went directly to a chair near the front door and took the robe draped over it. "April, honey, it's me." He would close the bedroom door without looking any further — yes, that was it, close the door. *Don't ruin it!*

But why was she still sleeping at this late hour?

As he neared the doorway he saw that she did not respond to his voice, and a sudden urgency flowed into his steps.

"April?" He could feel his heart pounding now as the menacing silence closed in on him. *"April!"*

He rushed to her side, not seeing the sensuous curves of her haunches as he stood over her, or the full, quivering breasts as he rolled her onto her back — but the smooth, undeveloped body of the four-year-old daughter he had abandoned in 1953.

"April!"

Her name left him like arrows through his heart, and he went down on his knees beside her bed and took her into his arms, holding her tightly.

"Oh, April. My God . . . "

But Justin Ross's long lost daughter was dead. Two hours now. From an overdose of heroin.

A tear-soaked note taped to her forehead read, simply, "Don't cry, Daddy."

The words were in Bullethead Cotton's handwriting.

Ross felt the pain ebb somewhat as he held his only daughter and sighed. He was a trained killer. He knew his craft well. But he was unskilled when it came to saving those he loved from the evil that lurked throughout the world.

It was her eighteenth birthday, but the Army lieutenant did not know that. Unless they involved the mission, he was not good with dates.

Epilogue

"Pro-Soviet elements have penetrated many key positions in the West, particularly in the mass media," father of the Russian H-bomb Andrei Sakarov was quoted recently in *Foreign Affairs* magazine.

Moscow spends over 235 million dollars annually to spread disinformation across the free world. That includes influencing high-echelon levels of the American news media.

In the spring of 1984 the founder and head of Accuracy in Media, Reed Irvine, recommended that the major networks investigate allegations that they had been utilized to disseminate Soviet propaganda. Despite support from other shareholders, Irvine was voted down cold.